Leaving Lost

by Serenity McLean

Leaving Lost

Published by Dome Tree Publishing

ISBN 978-0-9937314-8-8

© Serenity McLean, 2016

All Rights Reserved

Author's Note

Don't worry about anything;
Instead, pray about everything.
Tell God what you need, and thank him for all he has done.
Then you will experience God's peace,
Which exceeds anything we can understand.
His peace will guard your hearts and minds
As you live in Christ Jesus.
Philippians 4:6–7

Leaving Lost is a story of weathering the storms of life standing in the shelter of the Lord. The main character Samantha returns home to be with her mother who is fighting cancer again. She realizes she has spent two years mourning the loss of an illusion. She turns from drifting on a sea of hopelessness to walk on God's chosen path only to discover there are difficult times on any of life's paths.

Along with everyone else, I've struggled with bending my knee to God so I can stand in life's storms. I too have had difficult times which seem like insurmountable walls of stone, yet somehow God is true to His Word. All things do work together for good.

I hope this story encourages you to look back on all the boulders you've conquered and to stand boldly on your stones of faith.

Enjoy and blessings,

Serenity

Leaving Lost

Credits

Thanks to the many who continue to bless me along the way. As always I appreciate my family. My mom who encourages and is my biggest fan – love you, Mom. And my sister who is my best friend and always gently honest.

Thanks to my Hawaiian pastor JD Farag, for being my online pastor and contributing a message to the readers.

My great thanks to my editor Janet Dimond who both passed along improvement ideas and painstakingly pointed out all my errors.

Biggest thanks to my Lord who leads and directs in all things.

Leaving Lost

Contents

Leaving Lost

1 | Farewell, My Love

She had just enough time to stop and say a final goodbye before catching her flight back home. She stepped out of the car and opened her umbrella. The drizzly, grey day reflected her heart. Looking toward the back of the old church lot, she let out a deep sigh. For two years she'd refused to let go. She navigated through the cemetery to a quiet spot overlooking the River Don. She laid flowers on the grave and sat down cross-legged on the wet grass. It felt like it had been raining for years.

"I'm sorry, Andrew, but I have to leave. I'm probably not ever coming back so –" She choked on her rising sobs. She pulled out a tissue and held it over her eyes. Her heavy heart let out its pain.

Looking up the river she thought, *I'm going to miss this place, but I've held on too long to the past.* She ran her hand over the blades of grass remembering their days together – sweet days of hope and dreams.

Well, those sunny days of love are long gone forever. Death ripped my happily ever after from me.

She looked back at the gravestone, pulling her mind from what could have been back to the present. "Mom needs me now and I have to go. I guess this is goodbye. I love you, Andrew. I always will." She stood up, leaned forward and kissed the stone marker. She turned and walked away from her soul mate.

2 | Darkness Looms

Between flights, layovers and driving it had been nearly 20 hours since leaving Bellabeg, Scotland, or more specifically the little hamlet of Lost. Sam rang the doorbell of her parents' home in Hackberry, Louisiana, but no one answered. She rang again and waited. A sickening feeling rose from her stomach. *What if I'm too late? Oh God, I'm not ready to let go of Mom too. Please let her be okay.*

She waited for the taxi to pull away, then reached behind the light for the hidden key and let herself in. She called, but the house was empty. On the hallway table she found a quick note from her dad. "Hi Chickadee. I've taken Mom to Memorial Hospital. She's in a lot of pain. Call me when you get in. Love, Dad."

She picked up the home phone and tapped in the number of her father's cell. "Hi Dad. I'm home and I got your note. How's Mom?"

"Hi Sam! You made it home okay. Well, they've given her morphine. But she's still in quite a bit of pain."

"What have the doctors said?"

"They've ordered a CT scan, but Mom can't keep down the contrast, so they've delayed the test and given her some medication that should help manage her nausea."

"I'm going to change and come in."

"Okay. I'm sure Mom will be glad to see you."

"Dad – is this serious? I mean, should I be worried?"

"I don't know, honey. You know your mom. She only complains of pain when it's really bad."

"Yeah. Okay. I'll be there shortly. Mind if I borrow Mom's car?"

"Sure. The spare keys are hanging on the key rack."

"Thanks. Tell Mom I'll be there in half an hour."

Sam washed her face, tied her hair back and changed, then headed to the hospital. She remembered it was just a few years ago her mom was in the same hospital having emergency surgery to remove a section of her bowel with stage III cancer. They thought they'd got it all, but now with abdominal pain in the same area, all her fears of losing her mother rolled in once again.

She found her way to the emergency department and a nurse directed her to her mom. She peeked in. "Hi Mom."

Her mom opened her eyes and a weak smile broke through her strained face. "Oh, Sam." Her mom reached for her hand. Sam squeezed her the cool hand.

"How are you doing, Mom?"

Her mom looked at her for a moment drinking in her daughter's face. "I'm glad you're here." She closed her eyes, still weakly holding her hand.

The nurse came in to take her vitals. Sam noted her unusually low blood pressure and slightly low oxygen despite the tubes pumping it into her nose, and knew these were not good numbers.

Her dad held the cup of contrast for her mom to drink, but hardly had she taken a couple mouthfuls when it all came back up. "I feel rotten. I'm too tired. I can't drink any more of that stuff."

The nurse said she would call Radiology to see if they would take her without the contrast and they agreed. It was another hour before they came. Fifteen minutes after getting back from the test the doctor came in to talk to them. Sam's chest tightened, her heart sped up. She knew this could be the moment of distressing truth. They had been here before.

The doctor acknowledged her father. "Brent." He nodded at Sam, and then moved to the side of the bed. "Jessie? We've got the results back and it's not what we thought. With your history of bowel cancer, we suspected this might be bowel cancer again. We've found a lesion in your liver that has ruptured a blood vessel and you are internally bleeding. You're on a slow IV now, but we will pump in extra fluids to stabilize your blood pressure. I'll book you for a procedure to thread a wire through the artery in your groin up to your liver and plug the bleeding vessel. That should be in a few hours. With the extra fluids you should have a bit better pressure by then."

Sam asked, "How big is the lesion and what is its nature? Can you tell if it's benign or malignant?"

"It's a little under two inches. And no, we couldn't tell exactly what it is from the scan. Your mom's lost a little over a pint of blood and the picture is not clear enough to tell what it is. We will focus on stopping the bleeding first, then investigate the lesion afterward."

So it's not bowel cancer – a lesion in the liver. If this is cancer, it's far worse than I expected. Oh God, I'm not ready to lose her.

Leaving Lost

3 | An Old New Path

They took Jessie to the radiology suite to perform the embolization of her liver's ruptured artery. Sam asked her dad if he'd like a coffee. "No, Sweetheart. It's going to be two or three hours before they're finished. I think I'll find the chapel and pray for awhile."

Sam felt threatening tears. She nodded. He pulled her into his arms and held her for a moment. "She's in God's care, you know. He is the healer. He stopped the breast cancer and it never came back. He stopped the bowel cancer, and He can stop whatever this is. Just remember, Jesus paid the price of this through the blood He shed by the whip marks on His back. So, I'm going to the chapel to speak to Him again about taking care of Jessie today." He leaned back to look at her face. "Okay?"

She nodded again, taking a deep breath. He kissed her cheek. "I love you, chickadee."

She watched him walk away. *How I wish Andrew were here. I feel so alone – again. Where are you, God? Do you actually have any interest in us? Or are those words in the Bible just hollow and meaningless? I've lost two men I've loved and now again, Mom's life is in jeopardy. Enough already. Please – can this be enough?*

Sam felt restless and decided to find the cafeteria. She looked over the sandwiches, soups, hot grill and dinner options, but saw nothing appealing. She picked up a tea and a bottle of water and found a quiet bench outside. It was her favourite time of day when the afternoon sun hung low in the sky and bathed the world in golden warmth. She loved the way the sun beamed its peaceful hues through the trees, the warm cast of light on the buildings, and the way the shadows shifted from cool blue to inviting shades of chestnut.

She watched other folks pacing outside the emergency doors, talking to friends on the phone, smoking, waiting, stressing. *The hospital is such a world of hurt and loss. Even the gift of warmth from the sun cannot penetrate this pain.* She turned her back to the tension of the hospital pressing in on her, and focused on the small pond and fountain. Still restless, she wandered the winding paths through the gardens of the nearby park, trying to drink in nature's peace to fill her soul.

After an hour and a half she returned to the examination room to check if either her mom or dad had returned, but found it empty. She located the chapel and peeked inside. Her dad was quietly reading from his phone when it began vibrating and he headed for the door to take the call. She heard him greet her brother. "Hi Kyle." She fell in step with her father, listening as he talked.

"Yes, we're at the Memorial. She's in right now getting the bleeding stopped. She should be coming out in maybe an hour or so. No, no surgery. They are threading a wire up from her groin through her artery to her liver to plug the artery. We don't know. It's about two inches. They want to get the bleeding under control before investigating the lesion. That's great. I know your mom will be happy to see you. Sam is here. She came as soon as she heard Mom wasn't feeling good. Sure, here she is."

Sam took the phone. "Hey beach bum. How are you?"

"Beach bum! I'm no beach bum, you river puddler." She smiled at hearing his familiar voice and predictable reaction. "When did you get in?"

"About five hours ago. I dropped my stuff off at the house and came straight to the hospital. Did I hear Dad say you're coming home too?"

"Yeah, I should be there tomorrow morning. We finish our contract here in San Diego next week and I'd planned on taking some time off. So I'll miss the last few days, but that's okay. How about you? How long are you back for?"

"I think I've come back to the States permanently. I'm just not sure what I'm going to do just yet."

"Oh wow! I didn't think you'd ever leave Scotland! It'll be good to see you more often. I've missed you, you know. Listen, let's talk tomorrow."

"Sounds good. I've missed you too. See you tomorrow. Here's Dad again."

Brent took the phone back. He listened for a moment. "Okay. One of us will pick you up. Sure, text me the flight info. Bye."

He put his arm around her. "It'll be good to have my two kids home. It's been a very long time since we've all been together." He squeezed her shoulders. "I could use a coffee. How about you?"

They spent over an hour in the cafeteria. They talked about Sam's work in Scotland, Brent's work on the Gulf of Mexico and Kyle's work all over the globe. Sam carefully avoided talking about why they were at the hospital.

Brent looked at his watch. "Let's go find your mom."

As they turned into the hall of the emergency department, they saw the orderly bringing Jessie back. They waited as he positioned the bed and changed her oxygen feed from the bottle to the wall supply. Brent sat beside the bed and took Jessie's hand. "How are you doing, my sweet?"

"A bit better, I think."

The nurse checked on her oxygen and took her vitals. Sam noted the improved blood pressure. The nurse checked the bandaged incision they made to enter her artery. No bleeding. "Looks good, Jessie. You need to keep this leg straight for the next hour as you don't want to open up that wound."

Sam asked if the nurse knew how the procedure went. "The chart indicates the procedure went well. The doctor should be in shortly to let you know and answer any questions you have."

When the doctor stopped in, he told them they were successful in plugging the artery. They would be admitting her shortly to stay overnight for observation, and then would probably send her home the following day. They stayed with Jessie for another couple of hours until they found her a room then saw her settled and left when she'd drifted off to sleep. On their way home they ordered a pizza and ate dinner on the patio by the pool.

During a break in their conversation she looked at the pool and re-membered the endless days of friends and fun she and Kyle enjoyed there. When they were young and her girlfriends came over it irritated her that Kyle and his friends joined them to crash their party and jump in the pool splashing them. This always caused a sibling war. But once they'd hit their teens, having older boys hang around didn't seem so bad. She smiled, lost in happy memories.

Then memories of her first serious love invaded her thoughts – her first lost love. The pain caused her smile to fade. She pushed the memories away.

"I don't know if you want to talk about things, but did I hear you say you've come back to the States permanently?"

"Yes. It's time I let go of what could have been."

"What about the project you were working on?"

"I told my boss Rowan about wanting to come home because of Mom and thinking maybe I should come back for good. He thought it would be good for me. He said I was becoming married to a ghost and turning into an old spinster. He practically pushed me out the door. There's a junior gal who's been working with us for over a year and she can pick up the remaining work on the grant."

"Do you have anything in mind for the near future?"

"No, not really. Rowan has some connections back here that he's going to get in touch with to see if there is anything coming up. I know he'll give me a great recommendation. And I'll check into what's going on with the Department of Natural Resources and the university. Maybe they have a study I can join."

"If you want, you can run some charters. We're in the middle of a busy season. I'd be glad of your help, especially while your mom is recovering."

"Sure, Dad. It'd be great to get back to the warm waters of the Gulf. Scotland's North Sea is pretty cold for diving."

Standing up and stretching Brent said, "Well, I think I'll go to bed. I'm pretty tired tonight and would like to get to the hospital early and hear what the doctors have to say. I thought I would spend a bit of time with your mom before picking up Kyle."

"How about I pick up Kyle and you can stay with mom until they discharge her? Then we'll come home and wait for you both here."

"Thanks. That helps a lot. I think I'm going to like having you back home for a while. Goodnight, Chickadee."

"'Night, Dad."

Sam sat on the edge of the pool dangling her legs in the warm water. The dancing reflections memorized her.

It seems Solomon was right. There is nothing new under the sun. I've come full circle – back home and working for Dad. I've lost all I thought would make for a great life. Maybe I need to let go of any hope of finding my soul mate. Maybe I should move beyond caring and accept that life is going to be lousy. Maybe I need to plug my nose and wait for this life to be over before I can have a stress-free eternal life.

She heard the musical song of a summer tanager and spotted a beautiful red male at the top of a nearby oak tree. Several more flew in from the neighbouring yards. *A season of tanagers!* She smiled. Kyle loved to test the family on what groups of specific animals were called. Like a murder of crows or a herd of cattle, a group of tanagers is called a season. Her favourite was a tower of giraffes. Kyle's favourite was a wake of buzzards. *It'll be good to spend some time with him. It's been so long since we've seen each other. I guess it's been a long time since I've made time for my family. I'd been so absorbed with Andrew, I never saw anything beyond our love and our world. Then when he died I sat frozen, staring at the destruction of everything I wrapped around me for comfort. Two years and I'm over the desperate pain, but I'm not over the loss. My life feels like a big black hole filled with nothing.*

She watched the birds fly off. *Maybe I was meant to come home. Maybe spending time here, surrounded by the familiar, will overcome the emptiness of my life. Maybe the old and familiar is my new path.*

A deep breath turned into a yawn and she went inside. She fell asleep almost as soon as her head hit the pillow.

4 | First Stone

She slept in long past her father leaving for the hospital. After checking on Kyle's flight status, she drove half an hour from Hackberry where her parents lived to the Chennault Airport in Lake Charles to be there when he arrived. He was one of the first passengers to enter the terminal. She was surprised at how fit he'd become in his job as a commercial diving instructor. He hugged her and kissed her cheek. "Long time, no see."

"Yeah, last night I was thinking about how long it's been. It's good to see you. You're looking pretty smashing."

"Smashing, is it? How very British! Thank you. You look pretty smashing too."

"Horses for courses, ducky, horses for courses. You're such a stonking chap. You look cracking. I haven't seen you for donkey's years. How's that for picking up a little of the Brit culture?"

He laughed. "I understand only half of what you said."

"I said you may not be suited to British slang, but you are remarkable and look excellent. And I haven't seen you in a long time."

"Well done! Or maybe I should say, 'Spot on!'"

"Bob's your uncle. Do you have any more luggage coming?"

"No. I travel pretty light these days. The company will take care of my gear until the next contract. I'm ready to go. How's Mom today?" She answered as they headed for the car.

"I got a text from Dad saying she's doing really well today. They successfully plugged the bleeding artery yesterday. She lost over a pint of blood. They thought they would be releasing her today if she had a good night. How about you drive and I'll call Dad to see if we should go to the hospital or head home."

"Okay." She tossed him the keys and pulled out her phone. She briefly thought about the need to switch her service to something local.

"Hi, Dad. Yes, he's here. We're just leaving the airport. We're wondering whether we should go to the hospital or home. Oh great! Ask Mom if she'd like something from Steamboat Bill's for lunch. We can swing by and pick up some takeout. Okay. Is there anything you or Mom want or just get a mix of stuff?"

She heard her mom talking in the background. Her dad came back on the line.

"Got it. See you two in an hour with lunch ready to eat when you get home."

Kyle slipped the car in gear. "Steamboat Bill's it is."

While standing in the restaurant waiting for their order, he asked, "What are your plans now?"

"I'm not sure. Dad asked if I'd help out with the dive charters while Mom recovers. If you're around for awhile, we could run them together – just like old times. That would be fun."

"I'm home now until the next contract. I travel so much these days, I use Mom and Dad's as my home base. It's convenient for me and I think they like it when I spend time here."

"Do you have another contract coming up?"

"There are a few coming up. I'm just not sure which one they are going to assign to me yet. How about you? Are you going to look for something around here? Or are you looking farther afield?"

"I'm not sure. I guess I'll go where the work is. My boss in Scotland is tapping into his network to help find me something. And I'm checking on what research is going on through the university and the State. I don't know how hard it will be to get connected here again. Most of my contacts are in the United Kingdom. It could take awhile to find a research spot."

"I'll let all my contacts know you're looking. I know God will provide something."

"Yeah."

He looked at her for a long moment. "How are you doing, really?"

"Oh – I'm okay." She turned to look out the restaurant windows. "I'm empty and I feel a bit adrift."

"What was the name of the little hamlet you lived in? Lost?"

She laughed. "Yeah. They changed the name to Lost Farm for awhile because people kept stealing the sign, but they changed it back to Lost because of the uproar of the residents."

"So, you made your home in Lost for more than two years and now you've left, but it sounds like you haven't really."

She thought about it for a moment. "Like the song, I was lost in love. Now I'm just lost."

"You need to stop grieving over what's gone."

The cashier said, "Order for Kyle Morgan?"

He left her to her thoughts while he paid for their order. Once in the car he said, "I've been a bit worried about you. You're a special person, Sam. You need to stop drowning in your past. You are ignoring your present and future because you're still in your past. I think it's time you find yourself again." He hugged her shoulder. "I'm glad we have the chance to spend some time together. And I'll be glad to boss you around on the boat." Grinning he said, "Ah, good times."

Elbowing him in the ribs, she said, "You're not big enough or brave enough to be bossing me around."

He laughed. "There's the Sam I know and love."

Once they got home they set the table in the backyard for lunch. When Brent and Jessie arrived, they found Kyle vacuuming the pool and Sam testing the water. Kyle immediately hugged his mom. "Good to see you looking so fine, Mom." He bent to give her a big noisy kiss on the cheek, making her laugh. She patted his back. "You need to find yourself some deserving gal for all this lovin'."

"How are you feeling?"

"Pretty good. I still have quite a bit of pain, but the doctors say it is the leaked blood pooling and pressing against my organs. I guess it'll go away in time."

"How's the fatigue? Are you tired?"

"I think I'll rest this afternoon, but want to have a bite of lunch with my two babies and hang out here for awhile with everyone."

Sam stepped in and gave her mom a long hug. "Good to see you home."

"I can say the same back to you. It does my heart a world of good to have the two of you home. I've missed you, Sam."

"Well, it looks like I'll be around for awhile because I don't have a job now. Dad said I could work for him for the time being. So you're stuck with me for now."

Brent pulled out one of the padded chairs around the table. "Come sit down and rest. I see the kids have got our meal all set up for us."

Once everyone was settled they held hands and Brent prayed. "Dear heavenly father, thank you for your bountiful provision. Thank you for bringing the kids safely home. Thank you for dying on the cross for our sins and paying the price for our healing. In your Word you said that by His stripes we were healed. The healing work was done at the cross and today we thank you on behalf of Jessie for healing her again of this cancer. In your precious name we pray, amen."

Both Jessie and Kyle answered with an "Amen," but Sam remained quiet.

Kyle asked, "Mom, did the doctors diagnose the lesion as cancer?"

"Yes. They did a blood test and said it's primary liver cancer. They're setting up an urgent appointment with a specialist as soon as they can and that's who will work with us on what's next. I've reminded God of how we've made Him our refuge and He promised if we make Him our shelter, He will stop any plague from coming near our home. And now we just thank Him and watch His mighty hand work this out."

How could they stand unafraid in this continuing onslaught of primary cancers – breast, colon, now liver? This is so unfair. God, you are unfair. She has faithfully followed you without hesitation. How can you allow her to go through this again? She could feel bitter tears rising. Determined to deny her resentment from taking over her thoughts, she focused on the reflection of clouds and sky riding on the gentle waves of the pool until she had control over her emotions.

They enjoyed a couple of hours together before Jessie went inside to lie down. Brent, Kyle and Sam took the time to discuss the upcoming schedule of dives. Brent ran a successful dive charter for over 20 years taking folks on three-day trips to the Flower Garden Banks National Marine Sanctuary, about 100 miles south in the Gulf of Mexico and day trips to dive around oil rigs. Kyle and Sam volunteered to run half of them over the next few weeks. This would give Brent time at home with Jessie.

When the two men got on the Internet to talk about new diving equipment, Sam checked in on Jessie and found her resting, but awake. "Come on in, dear. Come sit with me for awhile. I'd love to chat with you."

She lay down beside her mom. "How are you doing, Mom? How are you feeling about another cancer scare?"

"I'm really okay. My life is in the hands of the great healer. Cancer has tried to take my life twice before and the Lord has stood beside me, supplementing what the doctors achieved in removing each cancer. Each time a new primary cancer pops up He ensures it is defeated. He has proven Himself over and over again. So if this is not meant to be, I trust this new cancer has no grip on my life. And if He has decided it is my time to go home to heaven, then I'm ready to start my eternal life."

Sam quietly fought back her fear and the tears of what she might lose. Her mom paused for a long moment, noting Sam's silence, then said, "Have you ever had an assurance from the Lord? Have you had a word of knowledge of something, and you just knew what was coming?"

"No."

"Well, I know this is not my time to die. The Lord has told me I will be here for something in the future that currently has no evidence of being possible soon. So I know this cancer will not win today."

Sam thought about her mom's faith. *How was it possible to believe without fear or falter. How did she travel so many miles of life and persevere with faith through breast cancer an bowel cancer, and feel she didn't need to worry? It seems I'm the only one worried in the family. I've tried to drum up faith by rehearsing the promises of the Bible, but for me fear always wins. I certainly don't have faith enough to stand up to cancer like mom does.*

Her mom broke the quiet moment. "So, tell me about how you are doing. Did you find leaving Scotland hard?"

"Oh Mom. It was so hard to lose Andrew. I really looked forward to our life together and then to have it all disappear in a moment – my dreams just vanished like a puff of smoke. I know it's been two years since he passed, but I don't want to let go. I don't want to forget him. Time has dimmed the love in my heart – sure, the passion has faded, but now I feel empty and I have nothing to anchor to. I'm just adrift. Kyle says that I've not really left Lost. I'm still there. I think I don't know how to leave."

Jessie reached for her hand and squeezed it. "You may still be in Lost, but coming home is a big first step in leaving the past in the past. Take your time here at home to find your footing again. You need to get back to hanging out with the living, not dwelling with your memories. You'll not find joy there. And hope lies in looking ahead. When you're pining for lost things you will find yourself a castaway in a sea of hopelessness. That's not who you are, and it's certainly not what God wants for you."

"I know you're right, Mom. But this is the second time I let myself fall in love and hope for a wonderful future only to have it ripped from me. I just don't know how to get over the loss and look ahead. In fact, I'm not sure I want to bother only to have it all ripped away again. I guess I'm scared to try again." Her breath caught in her throat.

Jessie wrapped her arm around her daughter, pulled her in close and kissed her head. "Oh, my sweet darling. Life isn't easy, is it?" She felt Sam nod. "You know, it's not any easier with a husband. Sure the problems are different, but it's not easier."

"So how do you get through with such hope and such peace despite such fearful things? "

"Well now, that is a good question. I can't say when I started out I was very good at standing strong and not letting life's storms batter me down. No, there were some very hard times where life brought me to my knees. But you know, on your knees is a great place to learn of God. I cannot tell you how glad I am of those early difficulties. Through those I learned that your father is not my rock or my anchor. Even as good a man as he is, he could never be the one I lean on. I know the princess stories of our childhood lead us to believe in a Prince Charming who will bring us happily ever after, but the truth is no man can ever live up to that standard. Jesus is the only Prince Charming. Only He brings happily ever after. My life with your father is a journey of two together leaning on God for hope and help. And that, my dear, has made our marriage a joyful journey. God is the only rock that offers all you are looking for – love, hope, peace and rest."

"But how do you get to the place of trust with no fear or worry? I don't understand how you can face cancer again and know without hesitation there is nothing to fear. How do I face life and trusting people again so I don't fear getting hurt?"

"It's not a matter of trusting people. It's a matter of trusting God.

There are some verses I stand on and the truth of them has never failed me. In Philippans 4:4 it says, 'Always be full of joy in the Lord. I say it again--rejoice.' And I'm sure that leads you to ask how can we remain full of joy? It sounds ridiculous to always be full of joy on this earth, but He will give you His joy, His peace. You don't need to try and drum it up yourself. Then the following verses on to tell you what to do to get to the place of trust without fear. 'Don't worry about anything; instead, pray about everything. Tell God what you need, and thank him for all he has done. Then you will experience God's peace, which exceeds anything we can understand. His peace will guard your hearts and minds as you live in Christ Jesus. Fix your thoughts on what is true, and honourable, and right, and pure, and lovely, and admirable. Think about things that are excellent and worthy of praise. Keep putting into practice all you learned and received from me – everything you heard from me and saw me doing. Then the God of peace will be with you.'

"I learned, when knocked to my knees, to pour my heart's fears, worries and aches to Him who already took all that and more to the cross. All of that misery died nailed to that old tree. I just need to tell my Lord how I'm feeling and tell Him I need more of Him in me, and He is always faithful in providing His peace. Then I need to discipline my mind to not dwell on the negative things that brought the fear, but to think on the truth of His Word. I look around and think on the beautiful things of His creation for me to enjoy. I think about what awaits me in heaven and I have renewed strength to stand firm.

"You know, you're not feeling anything Jesus Christ hasn't already carried to the cross. And by that I mean He felt all your loss, all your pain, all your hopelessness, and all your weakness. He let *all* of your misery and *all* of everyone else's misery fill His heart and mind *all* at once. I can't even imagine just all my life's pain compressed into a moment, but then add a world's worth of misery compressed and pressed into Him. Yet He took it all on for you so that this day you could call on Him and He would replace it all with His peace. And that is His precious gift. He died that you would have life and He bore your pain so you can go to His throne and have it replaced with His joy."

"So just pray about it and then think about good things? That's it?"

"Yes. It does sound easy. At first it will be really hard to train your mind not to dwell on the past and your loss. It's become a habit for you to dwell on the lost things. It takes discipline to bring your attention back to all that is good. And I had to ask the Lord for help with that part. But you'll find a life of unmeasured peace and joy ahead if you make the effort."

They rested quietly as Sam thought about the fork in the road that lay before her. *The easy path would be to stay locked in my loss. The other path is a hidden one. One I can't see past the first bend to the destiny. I'll need to trust what God said is true even for me, and Mom is evidence of that truth. It's hard to believe God will accept my prayer, help me keep my mind disciplined, and give me peace. I guess either I believe He will give that to me or He is a liar. And I know He's not a liar. So, the choice of paths is before me. I can stay on this known path of pain or I can make the effort to try it God's way.*

In her head she heard a still, small voice say, "Choose life."

"Where is that verse you just quoted?"

"It's Philippians 4:4 and 6–10. And the other verses I think will help you are Hebrews 4:15–16: 'This High Priest of ours understands our weaknesses, for he faced all of the same testings we do, yet he did not sin. So let us come boldly to the throne of our gracious God. There we will receive his mercy, and we will find grace to help us when we need it most.' In other words, He knows we don't come equipped with the ability to trust without faltering, and He's ready and waiting to help, particularly when we need it most. When the storms beat you to your knees, you are in the perfect place to pray for Jesus to step in. His peace is beyond human understanding. It doesn't make any sense that I'm not afraid of cancer, the grim reaper, but His peace is not of this world.

"You know, you can live your life beaten down to your knees by life, or you can choose to bend to your knees before God and stand in strength and courage through life's relentless assaults. Either way you will be on your knees, but if you choose to be on your knees before God instead of the storm, you will live in peace and joy. I've come to understand James 1:2 when it says, 'When troubles of any kind come your way, consider it an opportunity for great joy.' It truly sounds utterly ridiculous, but the wisdom of God is beyond our understanding. But because I've chosen to follow God's instructions, when life has dished out my fair share of difficulties, He has filled me with His joy – an abundant joy that wraps me in its arms and protects my mind and heart from the despair this world would like to impose on me.

"And so that's how I can deal with this challenge without fear. I've been in training a long time learning to trust God no matter what the world throws at me and no matter how dire my circumstances appear. He is gracious enough to shelter me in His peace while He works things out for my good. And I know He will do the same for you – if you ask and seek to follow His ways."

Jessie paused for a long moment. "You don't need to continue to feel adrift. There is a way out of Lost. You need to choose the better thing and commit yourself to walking this new and different path."

"I guess I haven't made much of an effort in my Christian walk."

"There's something I'd like to show you." Jessie opened the drawer to her night table and brought out a notebook with a cover of colourful river stones. "This is my book of remembrance stones. In here I write down all the things of my journey with God I want to remember – like all the times He's answered my prayers, or when He's revealed something in the Bible for me or when He's given me an assurance. I write them all in here. Then when life whips up a gale force wind and hail, I read through all my history with Him. I'm reminded of all the times He carried me and sheltered me. I read all the times He proved Himself to me. And I'm so much stronger when I read of His personal involvement in *my* life, not just the stories of people in the Bible.

"See the stones on the cover? Inside are the real-life stones that form the rock I stand firm on today. With every stone my faith is strengthened. I now count it a joy to add another stone to my foundation."

"That's really cool, Mom. I admire you, you know. I didn't really understand how you weren't getting all worked up about this new cancer. I hear what you're saying, but I don't quite understand it. I've never had a peace beyond understanding. Not ever. And I don't feel like I'm standing on anything firm." She thought for a long moment. "So you're really are okay with life's trials? You really think they are good?"

"Sort of. I don't believe the awful things of this life are good. Only that which comes from God do I call good. But I know God has and will work out all the bad of this world for my good. I am a far stronger person today because of His leading through the tough times. I have a lot of growing yet to do, but when I look back, these stones on my life's journey have given me the chance to grow in trust, refine my rough edges and shake off the bad bits of me. I could never have grown so much without the fire of adversity. I cannot say I like the testing and proving. But I like who I am when I emerge."

"Why didn't the church ever teach this stuff?"

"I don't know that they didn't. I find God's truth passes us by until we actually turn to Him in need. I remember when it finally dawned on me that God loves me regardless of the kind of day I'm having and regardless of the number of times I fail Him. Your father and I were in the midst of a family financial crisis and we'd been praying, but felt like God was silent and not answering our pleas. And I went through a time of trying to bribe Him thinking changing my performance would make Him love me more. I thought He was silent because I wasn't doing enough. Then one day when I was really seeking, His love filled me and I finally understood what the Bible means when it says that He offers steadfast love. And I sang "Jesus Loves Me, This I Know" throughout my childhood. Yet, I missed the concept entirely.

"In Isaiah 49:16 we are told He has engraved us on His hand. So my name is before Him at all times. Even when I'm having a bad hair day and

I'm cranky, He loves me just the same and is continually working for my good. I'd heard my whole life that God loves me, but only when I went truly looking for Him did I finally understand it in my soul and spirit. I now know He's never silent. He's already done what needs to be done on my behalf and just wants to spend some companionable time together. He worries about the problems so our time together is an investment in our relationship and not desperate begging and pleading. That was an early stone in my book of remembrances."

"You just seem so together and I feel so broken."

"We all start from the same place. If you want, you too can grow in faith and build your collection of stones as evidence of God's faithfulness and love. But a relationship with God requires you to invest in it."

Sam took a deep breath and let it out. "You're right. I don't want to live as an empty shell of a person anymore. I see who you are inside and would like to be like you."

"Would you like me to pray with you?"

"Yeah, I would."

"Dear heavenly father, thank you for bringing home the piece of my heart that has been wandering the world. Thank you for the life's path I've walked along that drew me close to you. I cannot thank you enough for gracing me with many stones that I now stand on a firm rock. You are a God of overabundant love, joy and peace. In your mercy you came and paid the full price so that we can come boldly to you and ask for your abundance to pour into our lives. Today is one of those days. Today, Samantha and I both come before you each with a big stone on our paths. We need you to step into Sam's life in a powerful way and heal her heart of the loss of Andrew, and fill her with your love. Turn her eyes to you so she sees her future with a bright hope. Fill her mind with thoughts of good things. Fill her heart with your wild enthusiasm for life and living. Move in her life so that stone on her path becomes a rock of faith. Help her build a firm foundation of trust in you.

"Thank you for your presence in my heart and mind today. I thank you for bearing the stripes of disease and destruction on the cross so that without hesitation I can ask for and receive your continued hand of provision in my life. So today I say, if it is your will may the burden of this cancer be lifted and thrown into the sea. Thank you for building my faith that I trust you will work things out for your good. In your holy and unfailing name, amen."

"Thanks, Mom. I'm glad to be back home with you."

"I'm glad to be with you too. I love you, my pet."

"Thanks. It feels good to hear someone tell me they love me. I love you too."

"Well then, it's good you finally came home. I think God used my health to bring you here. Perhaps that will be your first stone."

"Oh, I am ashamed if God needed to use your health to get my attention."

"Let me say it a different way. God loves you so much and He knows what I can handle. Through this we both gain a stone story. For me it is more evidence of His interest in my life to continue with me. For you, well, you'll have to figure that out for yourself. God always works things out for the good of those who love Him." Jessie yawned.

"Are you tired? I'll leave and let you get some rest. Again, thanks Mom for sharing such personal information. You've given me a lot to think about."

"You're welcome. I'll be glad to see you move past your loss and get on with life again. And yes, I think I'll close my eyes and maybe take a little nap. I love you so much and I'm so glad you're home for awhile."

Sam gave her mom a kiss on the cheek. "Love you too. Let me know if you need anything."

She found her dad and Kyle talking about fishing. With everything on her mind she had little interest in their conversation. "Hey Dad. Do you mind if I take one of the WaveRunners out for a spin?"

"You don't need to ask. Help yourself. The keys are on the rack. Take the one with the blue lure. It's for the WaveRunner. It's all gassed up and ready to go."

"Thanks."

She hopped aboard, steered out to Calcasieu Lake and turned south to a long, uninhabited island where she and Kyle used to play pirates. She landed on a sandy beach and sat down in the warm sand, leaning against an old driftwood log. A nearby oyster reef attracted a steady stream of pelicans, herons and oystercatchers. She drew in a deep breath of the warm, salty air and felt the comfort of home.

She watched the slow progress of a container ship fully loaded and heading south. She thought about all her mom said. *She and Rowan are right. My only friends are ghosts of the past – ghosts of what could have been. And that is the land of the lost Kyle says I've never left. And I've been afraid of leaving Lost. After two years of living in Lost I now see it is a place of hopelessness. And I could use a bit of happy for a change.*

She watched as a new bird landed on the little shell island and caused a ruckus of squawking, flapping and repositioning as the birds sorted out the new hierarchy.

What was it that mom said about my expectations? Oh yeah. No man can live up to the standard of Prince Charming. She's right. No one could ever live up to the stories of a prince riding on a white stallion come to rescue a poor girl and take her to his castle and live happily ever after. The more I think about it, it sounds like the story of salvation. Jesus promises to come riding on a white horse, and He does come to take us to His mansions and the abundance of wealth of the universe. Maybe the writers of the fairy tales were trying to tell a Christian message and over time we lost the true meaning. Now little girls grow up hoping to find a perfect man like Jesus to marry. Wow! That is a lot to expect of anyone.

And over the last two years the Andrew in my mind morphed into something beyond perfect. No wonder I couldn't leave. Who would want to leave the companionship of perfect? Everyday, my dreams were filled with a sugary sweet imagined future – my Land of Lost – what a trap of the mind. I let this snare seduce me into its beguiling attractions, but none of it is real or could have been real. It is not a place of fulfillment. It's a place of utter disappointment and longing. But every day I was intoxicated with could-have-been dreams and every night I was unsatisfied and craved more of the illusion. I've been lured further and further into this place of deception – this Land of Lost. Mom is right. I was adrift on a sea of hopelessness and didn't even know it.

The container ship passed out of sight, but the new racket of seagulls drew her attention to a fishing trawler. A cloud of insistent gulls swarmed the beleaguered boat.

She let out a deep sigh and closed her eyes. *It is time I leave behind these fantasies and fairy tales. They have nothing to do with Andrew and have nothing to do with real life. I've let this dream of what never could have been rob me of two years of real living. Yes, it is time to leave Lost.*

Dear God, thank you for showing me this deception that drew me off the path toward you. Help me step away from the seduction of this impossible fantasy of Prince Charming of the past. Show me the path to you and your pure joy and peace. Help me seek you for the satisfaction of my heart's longing. I do want you to be my rock and foundation. Soften my heart for seeking you. Like you said in the Bible, if I tell you what I need and give you thanks for what you've done, then you'll fill me with your peace. I'm pretty needy and I'm new to this path. I'm going to need a lot of help. Thank you for your mercy and grace to offer me all the help I need. Thank you for bringing me home. And thank you for mom's wisdom. I really appreciate all you've done in her life because through her experience you've shown me a path to life. In Jesus' name I pray, amen.

In her heart she heard, "This is your first stone."

My first stone – I'm going to get a journal like Mom and keep a record of my stones too. After thinking a moment she wondered, *What is my first stone exactly? Is it recognizing the crippling delusion of an illusionary Prince Charming and instead turning to God? Or perhaps it's more than deciding to let go of an imagined future. Perhaps it's about the commitment to change paths to the path of God's leading. My first stone I will label Leaving Lost. Yes, this will be the first rock on which I will find a first measure of faith. Thank you, God, for your help in overcoming Leaving Lost and for the seeds of faith you are planting in my heart.*

She opened her eyes and smiled. She felt a calm fill her heart and an assuredness about whatever was to come.

Leaving Lost

5 | Painful Points of Stone

Brent heard her come up from the boathouse. "Hi Chickadee. Did you have fun?"

"I went down near St. John's Island, down where Kyle and I used to play. Just hung out on the beach awhile, thinking about things."

"Your old boss Rowan called. He asked if you would give him a call either today or tomorrow morning."

"Okay, thanks." She looked at the time on her phone. "It's too late today to call. I'll phone in the morning."

Kyle said, "Maybe he's tracked down some work for you."

"Perhaps. Or maybe he just called to see that I got home okay. He's that kind of guy."

She heard noise in the kitchen. "Is Mom up? Why are you two lazy bums not in there helping her?"

Kyle raised his hands in surrender. "I tried, but she kicked me out. She said she's not an invalid. So I came back out."

She went inside to see if her mom would accept her help. Maybe it just needed a feminine touch. "Hey Mom. I can empty the dishwasher for you, if you like."

"No, no. I might tire quickly, but I'm glad to be getting back to my kitchen. Here, I've made some sweet tea. Sit and keep me company while I make dinner. I thought I'd fry up some plantain for supper. I doubt anyone is real hungry after the big lunch you two brought home."

"Mmm. I haven't had that since I was last home. Sounds good. I can help though."

The next morning Sam called Rowan. "Hi Rowan. I hear you called."

"Hi Sam. How was the trip?"

"Long, but good."

"How's your mom doing? I guess I should have asked that first."

"She's home from the hospital. She has a primary liver cancer lesion that ruptured an artery and it was the pain associated with the bleeding that took them to emergency. They've got the bleeding stopped and now we are waiting for an appointment with a specialist to determine follow-up treatment for the cancer."

"I'm glad to hear the crisis is over, but I'm sorry to hear she has cancer."

"Me too. She's actually doing quite well and her spirits are good. My parents are Christians and so they believe they are in God's care. Over the last decade Mom has had two other primary cancers and through medical intervention they have been stopped cold in their tracks. There's been no sign of those earlier cancers and they – we – are praying for the same outcome for this one as well."

"I'll keep you and your mom in my thoughts and prayers. I actually called because a friend of mine has a colleague and friend leading a two-part study right in your area. You live on the shores of, let me see, Cal-ca-see-ew Lake?"

"Yes, it's pronounced Cal-ca-shoo, but the locals call it Big Lake."

"Calcasieu. Okay. Are you near Holly Beach?"

"Pretty close. Big Lake drains into the Gulf of Mexico at Holly Beach. We live about 15 minutes north of Holly Beach in Hackberry."

"Okay. The National Oceanic and Atmospheric Administration (NOAA) is launching a project to develop a process to speed up the development of oysters to adulthood. I don't know much more than that other than they are looking for a lead biologist with experience in genetics. I told my friend about the work you've done here and she thought it sounded like a fit for what they want. She said if you forward your CV to her, she'll personally give it to the head of the study at NOAA. And I'll write a glowing letter of recommendation for you, if you're interested."

"It sounds awesome! Yes, I'm definitely interested. It'd be great to be able to work from home."

"I think it'd be good for you to put your extensive skills to work. This sounds like a perfect fit for you. Listen, I'll send you my friend's contact information. Her name is Dr. Pamela Acosta. And she said for you to get in touch right away if you're interested and she'd be glad to help you out any way she can."

"Rowan, this is fantastic. Thank you so much for this lead. I'll get in touch with Pamela right away."

"Yes, do. I think they are looking to hire someone within the next week or so. I'll get my letter of recommendation out to Pam today for you. Good luck. And let me know how it works out."

"Rowan, you are the best. I'm going to miss you."

"I'll miss you too, ducky. But I'm glad to help you pick up a great project. Take care, Sam."

"You too Rowan. And thanks again. We'll talk soon. Bye."

"Bye."

She danced into the kitchen where her family were finishing their breakfast. "Woohoo! Rowan's got a lead on a project out at Holly Beach. It sounds interesting and he's putting me in touch with someone who can put my name in front of the head of the project. It's with NOAA. It'd be great to pick up some work with them. This is fantastic!"

Pouring herself a cup of coffee, she barely drew a breath. "I've got to get my resumé ready and get it out to Rowan's friend this morning." She skipped out of the kitchen.

Kyle noted, "Now *there's* a bit of the old Sam back."

Brent said, "We'll pray that God will give her favour with the hiring committee."

By late morning she'd contacted Pamela and received a more detailed description of the project and the role of lead scientist they were look-ing to fill. She forwarded her updated resumé, a letter of application, and a personal note thanking Pamela for her help. They then talked on the phone. Pamela said she'd passed along her paperwork to Dr. Jay Patil. He asked if she could come to Lafayette for lunch the next day. He was very interested in meeting with her.

She was ecstatic for the rest of the day. That evening she thanked God for His help, knowing only His timing and provision could bring this opportunity to her.

The next day she drove to Lafayette. Just before going into the restau-rant to meet Dr. Jay, she prayed God would help her with the right words and that she'd be a good fit.

She liked Dr. Jay from the first moment. He was friendly and had the ability to quickly build rapport. They were chatting like old friends in no time. They talked through lunch and an hour afterward. When they were leaving, he shook her hand and said, "I think you'd be a good fit for the role. You certainly have the credentials and experience. The job is yours, if you want it."

She found it difficult to casually walk to her car and not whoop it up like she was at a football game. She immediately called Pamela and thanked her for her help, then took the chance that Rowan was still awake to call.

She did a bit of shopping while in Lafayette and bought a journal. She picked up a few new bathing suits, shorts and T-shirts, as she'd not needed much along these lines in Scotland.

Over dinner that evening she told her family about the opportunity. "Over the next month we'll get the team together, have a few planning meetings and get the NOAA requisite training completed. We'll start the project proper in four to six weeks. I'm one of two lead scientists. I'll be focused on the development of a fast-growing oyster. I'll be working closely with the other lead scientist who will be working on structural reef improvements to increase the success rate and directed spread of the young oysters."

Jessie asked if she'd met her project partner. "No, and Dr. Jay didn't have his name with him. The three of us will meet Monday and Tuesday at McNeese University in Lake Charles. They've got a room there we can use for the two days. And apparently the other lead lives in the Lake Charles area, so it's easier for the team to meet here instead of Lafayette. We will be going through plans all day Monday and Tuesday morning, then interviewing for research assistants during the second afternoon."

On Monday she arrived at the university campus early to grab a Starbucks for their meeting. As she stood in the lineup she spotted Dr. Jay sitting in the coffee shop. He waved her over after she'd picked up her drink. "Hi Sam. I see you have the same weakness as me. My mom says there's nothing like a good belt of coffee to get you going in the morning."

"Smart woman. Mine's a good belt of chai latte. So what's on the agenda for today?"

"I'd like to develop a high-level plan for both streams of work and resolve any potential timeline issues. We will need to clearly define what we are looking for in research assistants and review the resumés before meeting the candidates." He glanced at his phone. "Let's head over to the room now." He collected his files and dropped them into his pack. "Our room is across campus. I expect the NOAA boat to arrive in three weeks. Once it's here we can meet onboard. Until then we'll try finding a room here as we need."

They stopped at the admin desk to pick up the keys. As they turned the corner, Sam looked ahead and her heart seized. *What is* he *doing here? He's the last person I want to run into right now.*

"Hi Dr. Jay. How are you?"

"Good morning, Chris. I see you found our room."

No, no, no! This can't be the other lead on the project. Just when I thought things were going my way. Okay, think. I need to focus on the project and think about what this means later. Oh God, help me.

"Sam, this is Dr. Chris Chaix. Chris, this is Dr. Samantha Morgan." *Stay cool and collected. I'm not going to let this rattle me.*

"We've met before. Hi Chris." She extended her hand.

Chris smiled brightly. "Oh, we've more than met. We were best buds in our college days. Good to see you again, Sam."

Jay looked at the two of them. "How fortuitous that you two are friends. That should make working together much easier." He unlocked the door and led the way in.

Chris smiled. "We'll have to catch up over dinner. What are you doing tonight? How about a good crab boil?"

Her first thought was to decline, but decided it would be better to clear the air and lay some ground rules if they would be successful in working together. She glanced at Dr. Jay to see if he was listening. "Okay. I'm sure after today we will have plenty of planning work to do."

He laughed. "I was hoping to catch up with you, but I'm sure we can extend our meal and do some work as well."

Dr. Jay interrupted their conversation. "Okay. Now that you two have lined up your first date, how about we start with a quick synopsis of your related work to this project? I'll start. I've been the research director for NOAA for the last two years and before that I worked as a head researcher on several of their projects. Years ago I was a tenured professor at Duke, then moved to Tampa to become involved with teaching that involved more hands-on activity outside the classroom. I initiated a project between the university and NOAA studying shoreline erosion. Since then I've worked on shoreline restoration and disaster prevention through natural and man-made means. And now I'm almost exclusively involved in research rather than classroom teaching. I teach a double credit course each semester focused on my research. The interviewees we have this afternoon are applicants for next year's courses. This will give me an opportunity to see them in action before letting them loose on my research. Sam? How about you go next."

"I hold a doctorate in both genetics and marine biology. I've focused my career to date on invertebrates, particularly the most vulnerable. I've spent the last five years on a grant project in the U.K. to stabilize the failing populations of high-risk molluscs in both marine and freshwater. This included both genetic and environmental aspects for the European flat oyster, the critically endangered freshwater pearl mussel subspecies in Ireland and molluscs in the River Don."

"Thanks, Sam. I think you will bring a lot of insight to our project from your breadth of experience. Chris, how about you tell us what have you been working on?"

"Hard to follow after you two. I have a graduate degree in engineering and a doctorate in marine biology. I've spent the last ten years on State and federal initiatives to restore and protect shorelines and preserve intertidal and subtidal habitats. My last project focused on maintaining near-shore water at appropriate depths to protect upland banks and scarps against passive and active erosion in the Chesapeake Bay in Virginia."

"I think you are understating your work." Looking at Sam Dr. Jay said, "After working with Chris on an early headland protection project in Maryland, I've followed his work. Chris and his team developed a means of using natural processes to recreate tidal flats, spits and sandbars to encourage submerged aquatic vegetation to significantly reduce wave energy." Turning to Chris he said, "You also did remarkable work in developing an integrated shoreline management program for landowners to establish appropriate width dunes and marshes to protect shores against storm surge."

"Thanks, Dr. Jay."

"So, I think we are a formidable team bringing a wealth of expertise to bear. Now, let's take a look at a high-level plan. I want you two to look for fail points, as well as areas we can compress the project timeline and areas where you think we may need extra time. Be thinking about not only your individual stream of work, but also cross-stream dependencies and impacts."

For the rest of the day they laid out the work of the project and negotiated timelines and allocation of resources.

As their workday came to a close, Sam could feel her anxiety increasing about going out for dinner with Chris. She had to repeatedly push her worries out of her mind to remain focused on their work. Shortly after 4 p.m. Dr. Jay called it a day and wished the two of them a good dinner and a good time enjoying the memories of their "good ole days." Sam could feel her pulse and breathing quicken.

"I've made reservations at La Truffe Sauvage for 6 p.m. I don't know if you've been there before, but it'll be quiet and certainly good food. We can head over now and relax in the lounge until they have our table ready."

"When did you squeak in that call?"

"I know the owner and just had to text him. I can drive us over, then drop you back here afterward."

"No, it's okay. I'd rather drive there. Then I can leave directly for home."

"Okay. See you there in 15 minutes?"

"Okay."

While she walked across campus, she thought about Chris being her colead. *What are the impossible odds of this? Rotten luck! That's the odds. I wonder if I can cope working with him? We'll be working pretty closely once we're onboard. Can I handle that? Can I let go of the past? Can I wipe it all clean and start again?*

No, no, no. I don't want the flood of memories now. I don't want to remember my feelings and then go through all that pain all over again. Okay, tonight I must try to keep conversation to the present. We need to find a way to work on this project without resurrecting our tortuous past. This project is such a great opportunity for me I can't – I won't let him or my past feelings ruin it. Tonight I will close that door and just be myself.

When she got to her car, she bowed her head. "Dear Jesus, I know you saw this on my path. This Leaving Lost stone is so much bigger – lots of crevices and pointy bits, and far more dangerous than I expected. I don't see at all how this can be for my good. This is quite a test in trust. Thank you for Dr. Jay and a great project. Please give me wisdom tonight to keep our discussion to the project and current topics. Help me find a way to overcome this and be successful. Help me find your way to the top of this stone and enable me to stand on it. Help make Leaving Lost a stone of faith. Help me build my trust in you and your ways. In your name, amen."

With a deep breath out, she said, "Okay, I can do this." She looked at the time and realized she'd taken longer than expected to walk and would be closer to 25 minutes before she'd get to the restaurant.

She pulled into the parking lot and saw Chris leaning against his car, waiting for her. "I started to worry that you stood me up."

"Sorry about that. I was parked across campus. It took me awhile to get to my car."

"It's so good to see you again. I had no idea you were on this project. You look great, by the way."

"Thanks. I didn't know you were on the project either." *Otherwise I might have had second thoughts about signing on.*

"What do you think about the project?"

"I'm pretty excited. I think it's a great fit for me and I really like Dr. Jay. How about you?"

"Having worked with him before I can say he's great to work for. And I've been looking for an opportunity to work with him again. And now the chance to work with you makes it perfect."

Ignoring his comment she said, "It'll be a change from Chesapeake."

"Yes. It'll be good to be back home again. I've missed my family – Allison especially. I don't know if you heard, but she was in an accident a couple of years ago and was paralyzed from the waist down. She's been amazing though. She's so strong and upbeat."

"I'm sorry to hear that. She was always so athletic. What happened?"

"A really bad car accident on a rainy night. A truck lost control and hit her head on. It was 6 months before she got out of rehabilitation. She's very independent now. Her drive and athleticism enables her to look after herself."

"I remember she was always so passionate about horseback riding. Wasn't she headed for the professional dressage circuit? Is she still able to ride? I've seen documentaries where paraplegics are able to get up on the horse and ride."

"Yes. She still loves riding. Mom and Dad have dedicated a portion of the stables to helping her develop her skills. She hopes to open up the sport of dressage for other physically disabled riders. You should see her ride. She's still fantastic. Say, Mom and Dad are hosting a horse show this weekend at their Des Champs de La Baie stables. Why don't you come? If Kyle's in town bring him along. It's been a long time since I've seen him."

"I'll ask him. We leave Wednesday on a charter for Dad and get back Friday night. I'm not sure if he has plans for Saturday."

"You can come without him, you know."

She hesitated, wondering what to say. He pressed. "Come as my guest. I'll leave passes at the gate for you. I know Alley would be very glad to see you again."

"Okay, as long as I'm not too tired."

"Alley will be riding. She's pretty excited because this is the first competition she's entered since the accident. She has an amazing horse. Really, you should come."

"Okay, okay. I'll come. You should be her manager. You sound pretty proud."

"I am. I think the world of her and I'm so impressed with her determination. She hasn't let this diminish her sweet nature at all. I really admire her. How about you? You must be happy to be back home again. How are your parents doing?"

"Yes, it's good to be back home and Kyle's home for a bit too. He and I are going to be running a few of the charters over the next month to help out a bit. Mom has cancer of the liver that caused an artery to rupture. She was bleeding internally. She's home now recovering from that and we are awaiting an appointment with a specialist to determine what the next steps are for her. She's beaten primary cancer twice before, so everyone's pretty hopeful God will step in again."

"Too bad she's facing the fight again. Your mom is such a sweet, generous woman. I always thought she was special. She enjoyed having us hungry students over. I loved it because she'd make all kinds of goodies to eat. We never left your house hungry. You say she's beaten two different cancers already? That's pretty remarkable."

"Yeah. Mom and Dad really believe God has been her healer. He has guided their steps with the doctors and given them the wisdom for how to treat it each time, and once the doctors operated, neither of the previous ones has come back at all. They – we are believing in His intervention again."

"So God has been good to His faithful servant. That is a great story. I have many fond memories associated with your family. Your parents were always welcoming. Kyle was a good buddy. And although I started as Kyle's friend, I really enjoyed spending time with you."

"I think Mom loved having a steady flow of kids in their home – same with Dad. He loved a busy home."

He noted she didn't respond to his comment about her. "So tell me what you've been up to in the last ten years."

She talked about her recent project. He listened attentively, then said, "While your work is interesting, I really want to know about you. I want to know what that fun girl of a decade ago has been doing."

"Hmm. I don't know about fun. I found a wonderful Scot I fell in love with and in a few short months he proposed and I accepted. But he passed away a couple of years ago. I think I've come home to find myself again."

"Wow, that's tough. I'm sorry Sam. Well now, we'll have to make a point to have fun on the project."

"I know the research assistants will like that."

"Sure, but I was thinking we'll have to make a point of having fun together."

"I think it'll be important for us to include the assistants in all we do. It wouldn't be good for morale for us to not include them."

"I've been on plenty of projects where the team spends a lot of time on a ship together. I doubt they will feel isolated. In fact, it's just the opposite. Most people are looking for time alone. Too much time together in close quarters can accentuate bothersome quirks, making people edgy. Rather than a high-functioning team, you end up with each person becoming self-serving. What I was thinking is we could take some of our personal time and spend it together. But if you want to do everything as a team, I will try to abide by that."

That's not quite what I meant, but maybe I'm best saying nothing further.

"So now you know about what I've been up to, tell me about you and your life. Are you married with kids?

He laughed softly, but it faded quickly. He thought for a moment. Quietly, he said, "No, no wife and kids. I'd met the right person a long time ago, but she slipped away before I drummed up the courage to ask her out. Since then I've not met anyone her equal."

Memories of a cute blonde always hanging on his arm flashed through her mind. *No, this is not the time for these painful memories.*

He sighed. "I've dated quite a bit – at least until Alley's accident. I watched her boyfriend at the time walk out of her life. In his mind it was never a serious relationship and when Alley's circumstances changed, he just wasn't invested enough to stay in a relationship that then demanded a serious commitment. I don't blame him, but I saw what that did to her and decided I didn't want to get into the position where I needed to walk out of someone's life because I wasn't serious about her. Now I'm waiting for someone I think could be the right person before I get involved in dating again. God and I have had more than a few discussions about bringing me into the life of that special woman. I'm currently learning patience while I wait for His abundance."

"Poor Alley."

"She would be the first to say she's not poor. She had a tough time at first, but now she says it was all for the best. She never considered him marriage material. If he'd stuck around through her recovery, she would have leaned on him rather than leaning on Jesus. And in the end he would have been gone. Alley calls his leaving God's biggest blessing because as she says, "I now *stand* with Jesus.""

"She sounds remarkable. It'll be good to meet her again."

"She spreads her abundant joy to everyone she meets. She counts her disability an asset. She gets to meet a ton of people and share her amazing story of God's love for her."

"You sound like you're really into Christianity."

"I am. After Alley's accident and her boyfriend making a quick exit, she really dug into the Bible and we all watched a remarkable change in her life. She blazed a path to walking close to God. We all followed her and He's made a big difference in my heart and in my life. I finally understand what a relationship with God means and all those things the ministers said about Jesus now actually have deep meaning in my life. Out of Alley's struggle God drew all of us to Him. We now go to the same church as your parents."

Another example of God turning something hugely negative into something life changing. "That's really great, Chris. I'm glad there's a silver lining to her accident."

They chatted companionably for a couple of hours. She was glad he stopped saying things she felt she needed to deflect and redirect. Her guard soon dropped and she found herself laughing and sharing like he was a friend.

When they'd paid their bill, she led the way out of the restaurant. He reached for her hand to hold her for a moment to say goodnight. "Thanks for coming out for dinner. I've enjoyed our meal and your company. I'm looking forward to spending time with you – " He grinned. "Even if it includes the whole team at all times. Goodnight, Sam." He squeezed her hand.

She said a quiet goodnight. He looked at her for a moment, then turned to walk to his car. She stood for a moment watching him leave. He turned back. "Have a safe drive home and see you tomorrow morning."

"Thanks. You too."

On her drive home she thought about their working day together and their companionable evening. She parked the car in her parents' driveway. *When I saw Chris this morning and realized he was the other lead scientist, I thought my Leaving Lost stone suddenly grew a sharp point, but perhaps the sharpness is only in my mind.*

The next morning they put the finishing touches on their plan. By late morning they all felt confident they'd identified the risks and dependencies, and had come up with a solid plan. With a good feel for what needed to be accomplished, they turned their attention to the applicant resumés, selecting who looked most interesting on paper.

When they returned from lunch, Dr. Jay's boss Dr. James Finstedt visited their workroom. He was an older and weathered man who clearly spent many years on the sea. He welcomed Sam and Chris to NOAA. "This project is one that is dear to my heart. Dr. Jay has told me a lot about both of you. I agree with him. You three make an exceptional team. I look forward to seeing the results of your work. Oh and before I leave you to your work, could I have a word with you, Jay?"

When Dr. Jay returned he carried some papers he dropped on the table in front of them. "Dr. Finstedt brought with him the daughter of one of the major investors for this project. He would like us to consider her for one of the research assistant positions. Apparently she comes with a bonus investment of gratitude. He mentioned we are not obligated to hire her, but he would be 'most appreciative of the additional funds.' Here's her resumé. Look it over. She's waiting outside for an interview. Let's try to squeeze her in first."

Sam and Chris exchanged glances. Chris said, "It's been my experience that anyone or anything who comes attached with a bonus from an investor is probably not worth the bonus."

"You might be right, but it is a substantial amount of money. It would extend the project by another 6 months. So I think we should consider her."

Sam said nothing, but thought, *I agree with Chris. If her father needs to pay us to hire her, it sounds like a disaster in the making.*

They took ten minutes to go through her resumé then Dr. Jay invited her in. "Maya Treadwell, this is Dr. Samantha Morgan and Dr. Chris Chaix. They are the lead scientists on this project."

Maya was in her early twenties with a model-like figure, face and hair. Determined to not hold her father's money or her good looks against her, Sam decided to give her a fair opportunity to interview.

Dr. Jay asked her to start by telling them a bit about herself. "Currently I'm a graduate student at the University of Tampa in the marine biology program. I've focused my studies on ways we can leverage the natural forces of the oceans to our benefit. I was the lead research assistant on Dr. Grayson's study on the impact of invasive species on the Everglades. I was particularly interested in his work on developing genetically altered male mites as hosts to carry a rapidly destructive form of inclusion body disease targeted to the Burmese python to wipe them out. I would like to carry this work forward with my doctoral thesis on the powerful potential of genetics combined with engineering when I graduate. In the meantime, I'm interested in the research assistant role on this project because I think it would extend my experience in the use of genetics and engineering to help in the successful management of ecosystems." Pausing for emphasis, she continued in a low voice as though confessing to her priest, "I love Louisiana and hope to settle here someday. You know, I read about the loss of delta land and could just cry."

Sam was stunned to see her batting her eyes, and flipping her hair back, and noted the bright red polish on her fingernails as she rested her hand on Dr. Jay's arm when she professed her love for Louisiana. *Unbelievable.*

She asked, "Maya, you mentioned an interest in ways we can use the natural forces of the oceans to our benefit. I'm wondering what specifically you are looking to do in terms of extending Dr. Grayson's research on genetic manipulation of mites to control an invasive species. What direction are you looking to go?"

Maya squinted her eyes at Sam for the briefest moment, and then smiled. "I should think it is quite apparent. The Everglades is an ecosystem and I would like to utilize genetics like Dr. Grayson, combined with the strength of mother nature aided by the support of thoughtful engineering to restore the Everglades, a tropical wetlands, to its natural state."

"Yes, I understand the concept of what you are suggesting. I'm asking what specifically is your statement or theory. What natural forces will you try to leverage? How will you use genetics? What species? To what degree? What do you hope to achieve?"

"Oh, I don't have all that detail worked out yet." Turning back to Dr. Jay, she said, "I'm expecting to clarify these points with the work on this project." *Hmm. Sounds like she has no idea what she's talking about.*

Chris then asked, "You've mentioned both genetics and engineering. Those are two very broad areas of study. Which are you wanting to specialize in?"

"I believe a good marine biologist needs to have depth in both of these areas."

"There's a saying, 'Jack of all trades, master of none.' While all three of us have a doctorate in marine biology, each has our area of expertise. I'm wondering what is your intended area of mastery? It's okay if you haven't decided yet, but I'm wondering where you lean."

"Well, I'm a great admirer of Dr. Jay's work on shoreline erosion, so I guess if I'm leaning in any direction, it would be that one." She gave Dr. Jay her best winning smile. *Wow, I have never sat in on an interview where the interviewee so blatantly flirted with the interviewer. Wait, I thought she was interested in extending the work of controlling invasive species. Now it is shoreline erosion? She is some piece of work.*

Dr. Jay said, "This project has two streams of work. One, Dr. Chris leads the structural stream in which he will be developing a cost-effective and rapidly deployed means of supporting the propagation of oyster reefs. And two, Dr. Samantha leads the oyster stream in which she will be developing a means of rapidly growing oysters to sexual maturity. If given the choice, which stream would you prefer to work in?

"I think I would learn far more working with Dr. Chris."

"We are looking for research assistants that have knowledge and skill to contribute to the project. While there's always a lot to learn on any project, our prime concern is to bring on team members who can contribute in a meaningful and substantial way. From your resumé you have little background in engineering, wave mechanics or shoreline erosion. In fact, your experience seems a slightly better fit with Dr. Samantha."

She smiled brightly at Dr. Jay. "Of course I'll be glad to contribute where you see the bigger gap in the team." *The bigger gap in the team? She thinks my stream of the project has a bigger gap in expertise?* Sam fumed at the remark.

For the remaining interview she watched Maya focus all of her flirtatious attention on Dr. Jay. *This girl is going to be a real problem.*

When they finished the interview, Dr. Jay walked her to the door and thanked her for her time, promising to get back to all applicants the following week. Turning back to Chris and Sam, he said, "I think we just met a young Mrs. Robinson."

They looked at him blankly. "You know, 'Mrs. Robinson. You are trying to seduce me, aren't you?' – from the movie *The Graduate*. Maybe that's a bit before your time." He gave a resigned sigh. "What do you think? Can we find a way to bring her on?"

Chris asked, "Where exactly would we use her? From her answers it seems she doesn't know anything useful about invertebrates or genetics, for that matter. And she certainly offers nothing on the engineering and structural side."

Dr. Jay turned to Sam. "What do you think?"

"Based on her depth of understanding of the one research study she was on, she knows very little about research procedures. I agree with Chris. She didn't display any evidence of being able to contribute to either stream of work. And she appears fairly smitten with you, Dr. Jay. From her behaviour throughout the interview, I doubt she'll like working for a woman."

Everyone silently pondered the situation. Chris added, "I think Maya doesn't have the skill or motivation to carry her weight on the project. She'll need a lot of prodding, pushing and support – hardly worth the effort. But if you think Dr. Finstedt will pressure you, then is it possible to carve out a section of the project that is not significant and we can assign her that work? If there's enough in the bonus we could use it for her cost, and still hire an assistant for each of us."

Dr. Jay perked up at that suggestion. "What do you have in mind?"

"Well, could we put her in charge of general project admin? I'm thinking of things like posting and updating the project schedule, placing orders for supplies, doing our printing, getting in food supplies – things any grade school student could accomplish."

"That might work. If she proves more capable than we are expecting, then it will be a true bonus for the project. Sam, would that work for you?"

"Yes. That would free us up to hire an assistant we feel can contribute. If we do hire her plus two others, I think Dr. Finstedt will expect additional work to be accomplished. I suggest we hire very high performers for the other two positions."

"Agreed. I will see how critical it is that we bring Maya aboard, and if I can avoid hiring her, I will. Now, let's move on to our scheduled interviews. Which candidates do you think will be a good fit?"

They marked several resumés and began the interviews. They settled on two candidates they felt confident were a good fit for the demands of the project. Sam's top pick was Kaihono Kahananui, or Kai, who grew up working at an experimental mariculture farm in Hawaii. His family started a threadfin open ocean commercial operation with government grants. He then went into marine biology focusing on both genetic pollution in open ocean farming, and genetic enhancement and stabilization in a farming culture. Chris' top pick was Zach Northway who grew up on the Great Lakes. In his late teens and undergraduate years, he worked for the Michigan Department of Natural Resources as a labourer installing stone revetments and bulkheads. He started his graduate thesis on improvements to the construction of toe aprons to prevent scour from wave action.

When they wrapped up for the day, Chris invited Dr. Jay and his wife as his guests to the horse show at his parents' stables Saturday and reminded Sam her tickets would be waiting for her at the gate. Dr. Jay declined because of previous plans.

Sam drove home with a song in her heart. Despite the possibility of Maya on their project, she remained excited about it. About halfway home she turned her attention to thanking God for His provision. "I'm believing you have a path for me to overcome the dangerous bits of my Leaving Lost stone, like the Chris point and Maya crevice. I'm leaving these challenges in your hands, God. Give me strength and wisdom to deal with these and bring me to the place of standing on top, having conquered it and developed my faith. In Jesus' name, amen."

Leaving Lost

6 | A Lesson from the River

Over the next three days, Sam and Kyle took out three couples to dive the coral reefs of the Flower Garden Banks National Marine Sanctuary. The six of them were friends from Tennessee and made for an enjoyable charter. A flock of gregarious Wilson's storm petrels followed their boat out and a masked booby waddled around their deck looking for handouts. They were really excited to see a hawksbill turtle visiting the reef. Onboard they had a copy of the manta ray catalogue of regular visitors to the reef, which the couples used to identify the rays they saw while diving. They hoped to see a wide variety of marine life and weren't disappointed.

Brent met them at the docks early Friday evening. The couples thanked him for the opportunity to visit the sanctuary, saying they'd never forget it. On their short drive home to Hackberry Sam talked Kyle into going to the horse show the following day.

They arrived at the gates of Des Champs de La Baie stables at 9:30 a.m. and joined the long lineup. Sam was surprised at the size of crowd. When they got to the gate, the girl manning the booth gave them an envelope with two tickets, a program and a handwritten note inviting them to join the family for lunch at the main house.

The morning was dedicated to disabled dressage. Disabled jumping would take place in the afternoon. Late in the morning Sam and Kyle recognized Alley immediately as she rode into the ring. The announcer said, "Please give a warm welcome to Allison Chaix riding Dammerlicht. Dammerlicht is a ten-year-old Hanoverian from Germany and the pair have been riding together for four years." The crowd cheered and whistled as she passed the judges. She rode beautifully and the horse moved with gymnastic ease, dancing across the arena. They earned a standing ovation when the music faded. After acknowledging the judges and riding out of the ring, Alley paused to look at the crowd. "Go Edjers!" The crowd roared the same words back.

At the conclusion of the morning competition, Sam and Kyle made their way through the crowd to the main house. A posted security guard checked their identities before allowing them to pass. Chris' mom Jenny answered the door and greeted them warmly. "You look lovely, Sam. You look just like your mom. It's good to see both of you."

Chris came through from the back. "Hi Sam, Kyle. I'm so glad you made it today. Come on through to the patio. So, how have you enjoyed the morning?"

Kyle said, "Alley was amazing. In fact, all the riders are talented. I've ridden a horse a few times and can appreciate the balance it takes to stay on with all the changing gaits."

"Yes. I ride quite often, but don't come close to the skill of these folks. Most of them were pursuing dreams of the Olympics when injured. I think that helps quite a bit, but to ride as a paraplegic does require a good dose of talent and determination. The jumpers this afternoon are quite amazing. I tried jumping as a kid, but never got much above 3 ft. All the riders here today have dreams of going to the Paralympic Games when the Games committee finally accepts jumping as an event."

Alley appeared from the side of the house. "Sorry I'm late. I was talking with a few kids."

Kyle stood and offered his hand. "Congratulations on your win. I don't know a lot about dressage, but you and Dammerlicht were beautiful out there."

She smiled brightly. "Thank you. Dammerlicht is his registered name. It means twilight so that's what I call him. He's a great horse. Twilight knew right away things were different after the accident and he's been very careful and steady. He's had to learn all new signals for changes. He's such a smart boy. He makes me look good."

Sam said, "Great performance, Alley. You looked beautiful out there and Twilight is quite the dancer. And the two of you were stunning. By the way, what does Edgers mean?"

"After six months of rehab, I got back on Twilight for the first time. What an amazing sense of freedom that was. The next day I started a foundation to support disabled hopefuls for the Paralympics. The foundation is called ParaEdj. It sounds like edge, but it's the initials EDJ for equestrian dressage and jumping. We call ourselves the Edjers. Jumping is relatively new to paraplegics. Several associations and organizations are petitioning the Paralympics to include it as an event. Hey, we're hosting a dinner for all the Edjers, their families and our supporters this evening. Please stay and join us."

Sam looked at Kyle to leave it up to him. She expected his earlier reluctance to come would lead him to excuse them from the offer, but he surprised her. "That sounds great. Thank you for the invitation. We'd be happy to join you, right Sam?"

"Yes. Alley, it sounds great."

They joined Chris and Alley to watch the afternoon jumpers put in remarkable performances. Before the evening dinner and dance, all the competitors hung out at their trailers, making themselves available to the spectators and supporters to visit and get to know them. Kyle commented on how outgoing they were, and Sam added how they were so excited and deeply happy to be riding and competing. Getting to know the competitors made the dinner and dance a fun event. They opened the dance with a country line dance the Edjers had rehearsed. Halfway through the dancers invited more and more people until everyone was on the dance floor. Over the evening both Sam and Kyle danced with several competitors. The laughter-filled evening passed quickly.

Chris asked Sam to dance and kept her on the floor for several songs. She realized how comfortable she'd become with him around and gave a silent thanks to God. She commented on the impressive facilities. Chris offered to give her a tour and after the fourth song they headed out to the stables. He said his parents had built the stables and riding arena when he and Alley were young. "Alley was passionate about riding from almost the moment she could walk. She proved to be a talented rider, so Mom and Dad built up the property for her riding development, and for others to board their horses and take lessons. Then when Alley decided to start ParaEdj, they built the dining hall as a place for their use and for renting out to a wide variety of organizations. It's pretty busy because of the ease of access for the disabled."

Entering the stables he said, "They did a bit of renovation in here and to all the gates to enable Alley to function by herself. She's able to tack up by herself, and she's strong enough to lift herself up on the horse and get into the saddle without help. She's quite self-sufficient."

Sam greeted a few of the horses. She liked one in particular. With the horse nuzzling her, she said, "He's beautiful. He looks like one of those horses on the Budweiser commercials."

Chris rubbed the horse's forehead. "This one's my boy. His name is King. He's a Clydesdale, same as the Bud horses. I try to get out one or two times a week with him. I bought him about five years ago now. He was inseparable from his stable mate, so I ended up buying them both." A second horse popped his head out of the stall. "This is Eddie, King's best friend. He's a Friesian."

"You bought his best friend! You kept them together! Oh, that's sweet. Look at them together. Hi Eddie. You're a good boy too, aren't you? He's like Black Beauty. He's lovely – I should say he's handsome." The two horses vied for her attention.

"I see the two boys have good taste. Do you ride?"

"Not like you. I had lessons when I was young, but not much since then."

"I'll be taking them out tomorrow afternoon. I ride one out and switch horses halfway through. Would you care to join me? I'll give you your pick of rides."

Looking at Eddie she said, "Would you be okay taking me out for a lovely Sunday afternoon ride?" Eddie lifted his head and whinnied.

Laughing, Chris said, "I think that is a resounding yes. You have to come now. You don't want to disappoint him."

"Okay, as long as Eddie will be gentle with me. I'm not sure I'd survive a fall from that height."

"Eddie is very gentle and easygoing. You won't have any problem on him – or King, for that matter. Would 1 p.m. work for you?"

"Sure." She gave Eddie a final rub. Chris showed her the other horses in the stable including Alley's two. They left through the back doors and out toward the shores of Prien Lake. The moon sat low in the sky and reflected off the slow roll of the water flowing through the lake to the Gulf of Mexico.

"How come you never invited the college gang out here? It's absolutely beautiful." They strolled to the fenced edge of the field 20 ft. from the water's edge.

"It is, isn't it? I love coming out here in the evening. I love the sight and sound of the constant passage of water, yet it seems so still and quiet at night. It's like the water loses its restless nature for awhile." They stood quietly taking in the smell of water and the sharp calls of the common nighthawk overhead as it hunted for insects. "I learned a hard lesson in high school. I had a girlfriend that was more interested in money than in me. When I started college, I avoided bringing friends around because I didn't want to be liked for my family's wealth."

"I never knew you came from money. I just thought that life at home wasn't great and that's why you preferred to come to our house."

"No, our family life has always been good. I wanted to find friends who liked me for who I was. I had that with you and Kyle. And I soon came to enjoy your parents too. I really enjoyed the time I spent with your family. I guess I didn't want to risk the good friendship we all shared by telling everyone my family was wealthy."

Sam leaned both arms on the top rail of the gate. "It seems so long ago now."

Chris thought for a long moment, watching the water flow by. "Life constantly moves on like the river. You get busy, then look around and realize life has carried you a long way from where you were."

Sam nodded. *Yes, once bright opportunities of the past are long gone – left behind like distant cities of light. One bend in the river and they are out of sight. Life, like this river, gives a window of opportunity, then once we drift past, it's gone. Time to look at the opportunities of the shores of today. Time to grab what today offers.*

Chris pulled her out of her thoughts. "Ready to go back?"

"Sure."

On the drive home Sam and Kyle talked about the people they'd met and the stories of life they heard. Sam said, "I'm glad we went today."

"Me too. Alley introduced me to one of her good friends, Jonathan. The three of us made plans to go out to the pub for a quiz night with some of their friends. You should join us."

Her first reaction was to decline. But she remembered her thoughts about life as a river and her decision to grab the opportunities of the present and agreed.

When the pub night rolled around, she still felt reluctant. She thought about why an evening with new friends caused her to feel unwilling. *I think I've become comfortable in my Land of Lost. I wasn't like this in the past. No, I used to love going out with old friends and new acquaintances. Tonight I will break free from these ropes pulling me under the suffocating draw of the Lost – that illusionary place of fabled dreams. Now that I see what I've become – a shell of a person lost in an illusion that hid my devastation – I refuse to stay there. Enough of that sedated life. Time for real life and real people. Yes, time to overcome – time to stand a conqueror on the stone of Leaving Lost.*

Leaving Lost

7 | Pulling Daisy Petals

The next day looked like an all-day grey day – *all the better for riding. At least it won't be too hot.*

She met Chris at the stables promptly at 1 p.m. "Hey, Sam. Looks like a nice day for a long ride."

"Yes, it won't be too hot for us or the horses. How are you today?"

"Good, and you?"

"Good."

"Do you have your own riding gear, like boots and helmet?"

"No, I was hoping you'd have something I could borrow."

They picked through the equipment used by students and found what she needed. Chris already had King tacked up. "I wasn't sure if you would prefer English or Western."

"I used to take lessons in an English saddle. I was reasonably good, but that was quite awhile ago. If Eddie is really steady and has a smooth gait, I think I'd prefer English."

"I find him to be a nice ride and his trot does lend itself to posting. English it is. We can go slow until you feel comfortable."

He tacked up Eddie and helped her up. They walked out past the arena and onto a trail that meandered north through field and wood. It was wide enough to ride side by side and they chatted about horses, oyster reefs and life. She quickly got her riding seat and they opened up into a trot and canter. She'd forgotten the joy of feeling one with a horse, with the wind in her face. On their return they took the lakeside trail. Both King and Eddie enjoyed a walk through the water. *Now this is not the Land of Lost. This is grabbing the opportunity of the day.*

As they rubbed down the horses, Chris asked if she'd enjoyed the ride.

"Definitely! I felt like the shipwrecked kid riding Black Beauty through the waters of their deserted island. Thank you for inviting me."

"You're welcome. I enjoyed your company. You are a good rider. You have a good seat and quiet hands. I think Eddie enjoyed himself as much as you did."

"I think Eddie made me look good, didn't you, you handsome boy?" She snuck him an extra handful of oats, which he nibbled out of her hand.

As they turned to leave, Eddie stuck his head out of the stable and quietly whinnied. They looked back. Eddie lifted his head a couple of times. She went back to say goodbye. Chris said, "I think he's lovestruck. He's never called anyone back before. Now you have to come again or you'll break his heart."

Rubbing Eddie's face she said, "Is that how it is? Do you want me to come back just to see you?" He whinnied again. They both laughed at his impeccable timing.

"I try to ride every Sunday afternoon. You're welcome to join me anytime. Clearly Eddie likes you and it's good for both of them to have a rider. How about next Sunday?"

She looked at Chris, then at Eddie. "Okay. Only because Eddie is such a gentleman."

Chris leaned in and rubbed Eddie's neck. "Good job, boy. Thanks."

Wednesday evening Kyle and Sam arrived at the pub. Jonathan and Alley were already there with several others. It was an even mix of abled and disabled. Sam found them a warm and friendly group and settled in quickly to the banter. Jonathan had caught her midsip with a sharp-witted comment that caused a fit of coughing, sputtering and her drink to come out of her nose. He kept the conversation moving and everyone laughing. When she slipped out to the bathroom, she thought again about her reluctance. *I'm really glad I came. I'm actually having a great time. Yet another rope tying me to Lost is loosening its grip.*

When she returned to the table, she was surprised to see Chris. He'd pulled up a chair beside Sam's spot. He stood up when he saw her coming and pulled his chair out of the way to let her in. "Hey, Sam. Good to see you. How are you this evening?"

"Thanks. I'm good, and you?"

"Good. Did you get a call from Dr. Jay?"

"Yes, looks like we're meeting next week with the team. I understand both Kai and Zach have signed up and we are also bringing Maya on-board."

"Yeah, I was disappointed to hear about Maya, but at least we got the two assistants we wanted. Dr. Jay mentioned he wanted us to lead the meeting, so I wanted to talk to you about what to cover and dividing up the day." They talked for a few minutes about work, then joined in the conversation of the group. The evening passed easily.

When the gathering broke up, Chris walked her to the door. They stood outside for a couple of minutes, making arrangements to talk over the next couple of days as they prepared for the first meeting with the team.

On their way home Kyle talked about the evening for a few minutes, then went quiet for awhile. As they drove over the Israel LaFleur Bridge she thought about all that had transpired since she'd come home.

What a change a couple of weeks can make. I never dreamed I'd ever see Chris again, let alone find myself working with him. I was rather scared this would be very difficult. But God stepped in. Things are so much better than I expected. I've actually enjoyed hanging out with Chris. Maybe that pointy part of my first stone isn't actually so pointy. Maybe God has ensured a friendly project partner. We were once really good friends and it looks like we will be again.

"Look. It's a full moon tonight."

She leaned forward and looked up. "Oh yeah. It's pretty."

"It's funny to think every person in the whole world can look up and see that same full moon tonight."

"All the lovers are happy tonight. The darkness brings solitude and the moon offers romance."

"Where did that come from?"

"I guess it reminds me of a night a long time ago."

He looked at her, then left her to her thoughts.

A night like this so long ago – a night with Chris. I just cannot afford to let my heart get tangled in this friendship again. That went so badly last time. It must not happen again.

She looked at the river flowing by in the moonlight. *No, the opportunity for our hearts to fall in love is a long-past bend in the river. He's not even interested in dating until he's sure he's met the right one. This is not something I need to worry about. On the other hand, he's invited me to join him to horseback ride together – twice. He wanted to spend time with me alone at the Edjer dinner. We've been out for dinner together. God has brought us together. Maybe. No! I cannot risk this kind of thinking. This ends tonight.*

The next day her mother got a call from the specialist and was booked in to meet with the doctor on Monday. Sam felt a sinking anxiety. She'd intentionally not thought a lot about her mom's prognosis, but they would have to face the truth on Monday. She feared it would be a brutal truth.

On Sunday when she arrived for her ride with Chris, she didn't see him anywhere. She headed to King and Eddie's box. The saddles and bridles were hanging outside. Eddie spotted her and came to the door, putting his head out. She rubbed his neck and slipped him a carrot she'd brought.

"No wonder he likes you."

"Oh, hey Chris. You weren't supposed to catch me bribing him. How are you today?"

"Good. I've got a pair of boots and a helmet. I think these were the ones you used last time."

"Thanks. Yes, these are the right ones. Can I help tack up Eddie?"

They talked about the weather and the pub night while they readied the horses. He checked Eddie to make sure the saddle was cinched properly, then helped her up. They rode out to the same trail then took a side path. They talked about the project and the meeting with the team the next day. For awhile they rode in silence, listening to the songbirds in the trees.

Chris noted, "You seem a little quiet today. Is everything okay?"

She glanced at him, then looked up into the trees. She drew in a deep breath. "Yes. Well, no. Mom has an appointment with the liver specialist tomorrow. I know the odds of surviving liver cancer is not good, but I went on the Internet this morning to do a bit of research. It's really not good at all. I know Mom and Dad both believe God will look after things and can heal her again as she has survived cancer twice before. But I'm a little scared I may not have Mom in a short while." Her voice caught in her throat.

Chris gave her a moment. "I can't begin to know what you're feeling. I do know the road of the believer can be challenging. God asks us to believe in unseen things despite what we see around us – despite earthly evidence. Jesus said, 'Blessed are those who have not seen and yet have believed.' He said that to Thomas when he doubted that Jesus had risen from the dead, but I think there is a blessing for all of us who believe in His promises when the earthly evidence indicates the opposite. The Lord will bless your parents for their trust. Do you want me to pray with you about your concerns?"

She nodded, afraid to say anything for fear of bursting into tears.

He stopped the horses and had King stand beside Eddie. He reached over and took her hand. "Dear heavenly father, our God who knows the journey of our life even before we are born. You know what lies ahead for Jessie with her diagnosis of cancer. We know you have intervened twice before and guided the surgeons to effectively remove all traces of it. We give you the glory for imparting your wisdom to her doctors. We come again asking for your help. We pray that the specialist Jessie will meet with tomorrow will confidently know how to treat the cancer and you will bring all things together for good like you did with Alley's accident. And I also pray you would comfort Sam today. You are the great comforter. We ask that you would fill her with your hope and joy and remove her fear. As King David said in Psalm 33, 'Our hope lies in your steadfast love.' Give Sam peace about her mom's life – a peace beyond understanding. Make your presence known to Sam even now. Show her that you walk alongside and she can lean on you. Fill her with the comfort of knowing you will never leave her. All this we pray according to your Word. In your name of truth, light and life we pray, amen."

She wiped away her tears. "Amen. Thank you, Chris. That was perfect."

"Look up. See that songbird in the tree there? God cares for even that bird, that it would have food, water and shelter. How much more He cares for you, a woman who is called of God, and we know God works out everything for the good for those who love Him."

With new tears brimming in her eyes she, looked at him and nodded. "You are very kind. Thank you. I'll be okay."

"Okay, let's go. I think the horses are getting a little restless. There's something up ahead I want to show you."

They rode on another few minutes, then the woods opened to a patch of grassy land. An old building with a metal roof and peeling paint stood sagging under the weight of time.

"What is it?"

"It's an old blacksmith shop from a long-lost plantation. There's still an anvil in there and you can see the forge."

He helped her down and they peered in the dusty windows. "Too bad it's tucked way out here where no one can see it."

They wandered around the building. "Do you know when it was built?"

"I've heard it's from the mid-1800s."

"Wow. And it's still standing. Thanks for showing me. It's a historical treasure just hidden away."

He helped her back up on Eddie, got on King and turned to continue down the trail. She took one final look, then turned to follow him. "Just think. That building has served people for over 150 years. And even though we've forgotten about it, and grass and trees are closing in, it still stands. In and out of favour, it stands. I'd like to grow old like this building. Still standing regardless of whether people still value me or even know about me."

Chris looked at her, wondering what in her life would elicit such a thought. "It does have an air of nobility for its age. And I hope I'll carry myself with such nobility despite my wrinkles and sagging frame when I get old."

She laughed. "I can't picture you as an old wrinkled prune."

He puffed out his chest. "I'll take that as a compliment. But I think that's why God gives us grandparents – to remind us where life will inevitably take us. Best we don't get too full of ourselves. I guess if we serve a good purpose in our youthful strength, like that old building, we can stand proud in our old age despite the weathered body."

"Maybe we should go back and I'll take a picture. Then when you get old, I'll remind you of this noble weathered building standing proud."

He laughed. "Is that a promise? You're going to be around in my old age?"

"I guess I'll have to be if I'm going to remind you of your nobility."

"Sounds good to me. I thought I'd lost you forever and now you're back promising to be around right through to my old age."

"Wait a minute. I said I'd be happy to remind you of your youth when you're old. Didn't say anything about the time in-between."

"No, no. You said you'd be around and I'm going to hold you to that promise."

She smiled and shook her head at his teasing. "What I will promise is that I'll be around for the length of the project."

"Oh, I see so much further into our future and we go beyond the project."

"Whatever."

He laughed.

They rode back along the river, giving the horses a chance to cool off in the water. After brushing the horses down and ensuring they had plenty of water and feed, Chris invited her for an early dinner.

When driving home over the bridge, she was reminded of her thoughts on the night of the full moon. That night she thought the time for a relationship with Chris was long past. *The attention he's paid me over the last couple of weeks might suggest interest anew. I wonder if my life's river is giving me another swing by that long-past opportunity. There's a lot to like about Chris. There's always been a lot to like about him. Maybe now that we are both more mature it would be okay. He did say he wouldn't date again unless he thought it could be something long lasting. But then, does he consider horseback riding and dinner a date? He's never said anything that would make me think it's a date. No, it's best to keep it at a friendship. I don't want another heartbreak on my hands. We need to get through the project, then sort out what this is.*

Walking into the house she spotted her mom's potted daisies at the door and was reminded of the childhood game of pulling the petals off. *He loves me. He loves me not. A child's game and yet here I am playing it again. Chris loves me. He loves me not. I will put that all behind me. There's time at the end of the project to sort out if there's any possibility of a lifelong relationship. For now I need to keep my attention on finding the way to standing in faith on top of my Leaving Lost stone.*

8 | A Ray of Sunshine

Monday passed slowly for Sam. The day with the team was mostly good. Maya was predictably flirtatious with Dr. Jay. Sam comforted herself with the thought that generally Dr. Jay wouldn't be on the boat with them. She hoped without his presence Maya might function as a respectful and responsible team member.

She'd managed to put away her worries about the specialist's prognosis. She resisted the urge to call or text to find out how things went. She decided it would be best not to be at work when she heard the news. It was hard to drive home without speeding. As her anxiety rose so did her speed. She'd catch herself and ease off the gas pedal only to find herself speeding a couple minutes later.

When she pulled into the driveway, she drew in a deep breath and prayed for courage before getting out. She could hear laughter coming from the backyard. She walked around the side to find her parents and Kyle around the table. Kyle called out a hello to her, then dashed into the house.

Jessie saw her coming. "Hi dear. How was your day?"

She kissed her mom's cheek. "It was good. More importantly, how was yours? How did it go with the specialist?"

"They did a couple of tests and said I have a very healthy liver – no cirrhosis and no hepatitis. Apparently it's rare to have primary liver cancer and even more so with a healthy liver. There is only the one lesion, which is good. He said if I'd come to him before the bleeding, he would have recommended they treat it exactly how they treated the bleeding – by plugging the bleeding artery and letting the cancer tissue die. He looked at the MRI after they plugged the artery and said it looks like all of the cancer has died. There is a ring of tissue that could be remnant cancer cells, but it also could be inflamed liver cells. So I'm going back in three months for a follow-up MRI and appointment with the doctor to confirm there is no more cancer, and if it's growing again, there are several options to address it that don't involve surgery."

Her father said, "Again, the Lord has stepped in and guided the doctor to plug the artery in such a way that eliminated the cancer. We were waiting for you to come home to celebrate the good news."

"Oh Mom. I'm so happy for you. This is great news! I didn't know if you'd need a big surgery or what."

Kyle returned with a cherry and whipped cream extravaganza with lit candles. Her father served each of them a large slice. "Tonight it doesn't matter if we spoil our appetites."

This is the first really good day I've had for a very long time. Thank you, God, for bringing sunshine into my life. Your path is a far sunnier one than the one in Lost. I think I can see the top of my first stone. And maybe the pointy bits aren't so pointy. I'm going to mark this as a day of God's grace in my prayer journal.

9 | An Open Door

The next few weeks passed easily. Sam and Kyle handled three charters for their dad. They joined the pub gang a few times, enjoying their fun and laughter. And she went riding several times with Chris. She always loved her time in nature and made the most of her time diving. She equally enjoyed riding through the woods and fields. Eddie proved to be a horse full of personality and a good mount. It had been six weeks since coming home. With her new friends and activities, she'd come to feel she belonged again. She started to feel firm ground under her and not so lost and adrift.

On the Sunday of her seventh week home, Chris invited the team to his parents' place for a little team building. He planned a trail ride, then a barbequed steak dinner on their back patio. Maya arrived rather put out about participating, then with one look around Des Champs de La Baie she initiated mission flirtation. She hovered around Chris telling him she'd not ridden before. Flipping her hair she told him she'd need his help. Giggling she commandeered his time answering her endless questions. To Chris's credit, he patiently handled her incessant distraction while ensuring horses and people were properly geared up and ready for the ride.

Sam had ridden several times with Chris and offered to bring up the rear. Maya stuck like glue to him. The two lads Zach and Kai divided their time between Chris and Sam and each other. Zach proved to have a wonderful sense of humour and the two lads hit it off, making fun for the team. Other than Maya's sudden attraction to Chris and her dismissive attitude to the lads, they had a pleasant afternoon together. When back at the stables the lads both helped with removing the tack and brushing down their horses. Maya nattered at Chris while he took care of her horse for her.

Over dinner her divisive and dismissive attitude became quite clear. Both the lads stopped trying to include her in conversation. Sam watched as Chris tried to dodge Maya and spend some time with the lads. With every move she seemed to be front and centre. She tried hard to press Chris into taking her back to the university where she was staying, but the lads intervened and she finally left with them.

The following morning Chris picked Sam up and they drove to the coast to meet the team. The research vessel *Manta* had docked at the marina in Cameron late Sunday. Normally it patrolled the reefs of the Flower Garden Banks National Marine Sanctuary, but was made available for the length of their project. The first week they would be making scans of the shoreline and shallow waters. Sam would be collecting samples of oysters, water and taking a wide variety of air, wind and water readings. They expected to be out at the sanctuary the following week. While the team worked in the labs, the *Manta* crew would patrol the reefs of the sanctuary.

They met Captain Darrel, one of the two captains of the *Manta*, and two crew members Paul and Jason. Darrel conducted the orientation to the onboard equipment as well as safety procedures. In an hour and a half they were underway to begin their slow cruise of the coast east of Holly Beach.

The project included the coast all the way to Atchafalaya Bay including Vermilion Bay, about 400 miles of shoreline.

Sam, Kai and Maya spent the bulk of the day in the rigid hull inflatable boat called a RHIB. Kai and Sam collected a wide variety of samples and Maya monitored the machines collecting water, air and wind readings. They met up with the *Manta* in the late afternoon loaded with samples and data from ten existing oyster reefs. From what Sam could tell most were in decline and she and Kai would need to do a bit of detective work to identify the cause before tackling the challenge of cutting the time to maturity.

Over dinner the team and crew divided up the cooking and kitchen cleanup duties for the next few weeks. They would work in pairs with each person buddied up with someone different each time they came on duty. Maya took the opportunity of a captive audience to talk about her previous research study. The lads politely asked a couple of questions. When she suggested their questions showed a lack of understanding, they realized Maya did not want a dialogue. As soon as the meal was finished, the lads excused themselves. Sam was determined to try to make Maya feel a part of the team and asked about her school year. She answered, but when Chris said he wanted to stretch his legs on deck, Maya quickly finished her answer and skipped out after him.

Sam watched her disappear and decided to head to the upper deck. There were seats at the fore that gave a great view of the ocean. It was dusk and the sunset extending across the Gulf painted in pinks and oranges took her breath away. A few minutes later Kai joined her. They sat quietly for several minutes. They could hear the sound wind makes on feathers as a pelican flew over the deck. It circled nearby, then dove down, tucked in its wings and plunged into the waves. It popped up floating on the surface, tossed its head up and gulped down a fish. He said, "I've missed being on the water while in school. I've always enjoyed bird visitors. My favourites are the moli who endlessly float on air and the 'ua'u kani who dive-bomb and swim underwater after fish. I think our threadfin ocean farm is on the must-see tour list for all of the fish-hunting birds of Hawaii."

"I've never heard of those kinds of birds."

"Sorry, I'm so used to the Hawaiian names. Moli are a species of albatross and 'ua'u kani are shearwaters."

They chatted about the workings of the farm and his family. Zach wandered to the upper deck and joined the conversation. They watched the sun go down and the first stars come out. Sam found the lads easygoing, decided they would be a pleasure to work with, and expected they would make the time in close quarters go smoothly. As she headed to bed, she saw Maya still talking to Chris. *That girl doesn't know the value of quiet.*

The week passed much like the first day. The lads and Sam often spent their evenings together on the upper deck learning Hawaiian, sharing funny stories and talking about the project. She felt a bit sorry for Chris, as Maya never gave him a spare moment to himself.

Thursday was Maya's turn in the kitchen with Kai. After dinner Zach had a Skype date with his girlfriend. Sam went to her usual upper deck retreat. She noticed a pod of dolphins playing around the boat. She headed to the lower deck to lean over and watch. Chris came out with his coffee and joined her.

"Looks like the kids are all busy tonight."

Sam laughed. "I notice one of the kids is rather taken with you."

"Yeah, I think she's just lonely."

"That isn't quite the word I'd have chosen."

"What word would you use?"

"Well, if she were truly lonely, she would welcome Kai, Zach and I into the conversation. The lads are quite friendly and have tried to reach out to her. But she only has eyes for you."

"I don't know about that. I guess I feel sorry for the kid. She said her mom left when she was barely out of diapers and her dad has little time for her. He's paid people to take her off his hands her whole life. It can't have been easy and I can understand why she is the way she is. I think we can give her a taste of what it's like when she's a valued member of the team."

"That indeed is a tough childhood, but be careful, Chris. I don't think a difficult upbringing exactly explains her current behaviour. I don't know if you've noticed, but she is successfully separating you from the rest of us. She really doesn't want anyone else around you but her. Just be careful, okay?"

"Oh, I don't think there's anything to worry about. She just feels that the lads, as you call them, don't like her."

"I think they don't like the way she's dividing us into two groups. I'm sure Zach would enjoy a bit more of your time. We often talk about the project in the evening, between learning Hawaiian words and playing punch buggy bird. Maybe you two could join us. We hang out on the upper deck to watch the sunset."

"Punch buggy bird? What's that?"

"You know the kids' game punch buggy where they punch each other on the arm when they see a Volkswagen Beetle? It's kind of like that. Only you need to look for different kinds of birds we haven't seen that evening. You have to identify the type of bird when punching. You get a double punch if the bird is diving in the water."

They stood leaning on the rail of the deck. A red-footed booby flew by. "So like, punch buggy booby!" and she punched him on the shoulder. She looked back toward the distant shore and spotted a pelican. "Punch buggy pelican!"

Laughing and rubbing his shoulder, he said, "Okay, okay. I get it. It sounds like you are having fun with the lads."

"They are great guys. The crew and Darrel have joined us on a couple of evenings. I think it'd be good for the team if you joined in."

He looked out to sea for a long moment. "I've heard you guys laughing. I tried encouraging Maya to join in, but she seems reluctant. I'll try again. You're right. It is good for the team to play together as well as work together."

They talked for awhile longer as heavy grey clouds pressed in. With incoming rain they went to the wheelhouse to check on the weather forecast for the next day. Darrel was looking at the readout from the onboard weather station. He looked up when they entered. "Looks like a long, lingering storm, I'm afraid. You are in for a full day of rain tomorrow."

"Will it be too rough to collect data?"

"No, I would expect a light wind, if anything. These are low, slow clouds that will just hang here and dump rain all day. It'll be a bit cooler. You'll want either rain gear or wetsuits."

She poked Chris in the ribs. "*We'll* need rain gear. You and Zach will be sitting comfortably dry inside."

"Yeah? We've been stuck onboard while you guys have been out in the sun and surf every day."

Darrel laughed. "All's fair in love and war."

She said, "Thanks for backing me up, Darrel. No dessert for you next time I'm in the kitchen. And I was going to make a batch of peanut butter cookies just for you."

"Hey, hey. Not the peanut butter cookies. You know how to hit a guy where it hurts."

"You did say, 'All's fair.'"

"Yeah, I meant between you two. Did I mention that I feel bad for you having to spend the day in the rain?"

She laughed. "Okay! Peanut butter cookies for you."

Chris shook his head. "Man, you caved way too easily."

"Love my peanut butter cookies. What can I say?"

She rested her hand on Darrel's shoulder. "Don't worry. I'll keep you in cookies for the length of the project."

He closed his eyes and smacked his lips. "You're my most favourite scientist ever."

"You probably say that to all the scientists."

"Only the ones who make cookies."

Chris said, "Okay, I see how this is going." With a fake serious tone, he pointed at Sam. "Two can play this game. You want war? You got it."

She laughed. "What? Are you going to get your mom to bake something?"

"No. Way better than that."

Darrel rubbed his stomach. "I like the way this is going."

While Chris and Darrel bantered on, she thought, *God, I know you've put such good men in my life. They make it easy to let go of the past and live in the present. Thank you for putting good people on my path – good people that draw me back to the land of the living, not the land of the lost.* The conversation moved on to scheduling logistics.

The team took Friday evening through to Sunday afternoon as their weekend. New clouds blew in on Sunday morning. By noon a steady drizzle promised to last well into the night. The team boarded late afternoon to give time for the *Manta* to head to the reefs. Chris and Paul were busy in the kitchen prepping dinner. With it raining outside the lads and Sam gathered in the mess. Kai discovered the games cupboard. "Anyone interested in a game of Scrabble or Yahtzee or Monopoly?"

Zach and Sam settled on Monopoly. Sam said, "How about we invite Maya to join us?"

"I doubt she has any interest in playing any game with us."

"You don't know that. Listen, she's had a tough childhood. Her mom left her when she was a toddler and her dad made no time for her. The least we can do is ask her."

Kai said, "Is that what she said? What a crock! I've seen photos of her and her mom in her Instagram feed. And I know it's her mom because she is a much younger version of her mom. She's no abandoned orphan."

Zach said, "I know a guy that was on her other project – the project she's always talking about. He said she was exactly the same there – slamming her teammates and isolating Dr. Grayson from the team, commandeering all of his spare time. He said she ended up getting dismissed from the project because of her misbehaviour with Grayson. She almost got expelled. She came into his room one night wearing only a little bit of lingerie. Later she claimed he insisted on an amorous rendezvous for grades, which he denied. The team backed him up and she was punted off the project and out of the course. She's bad news. I'm just glad she hasn't turned her attention to me."

Kai said, "That won't happen. She has no interest in you or I. Neither of us runs the show. She's the sort that goes after the big game."

"True. Anyway, that's why we steer clear of her. And whatever story she's told about her father or mother abandoning her is just that – a fairy tale. I don't believe much of what she says."

"Hmm. Thanks for telling me all this. It does suggest we take care, but we still need to operate as a team. I appreciate that you haven't let her past interfere with pulling together to complete the research." The conversation then turned to the project and the upcoming week of data analysis.

Jason wandered in as they were setting up for the game. "Hey, got room for another player?"

Zach said, "Only if you want a good whoopin'."

"You research guys are all the same." In a falsetto voice he said, "Oh, I'm so good at Monopoly. No one else is as good as me." In his normal voice he said, "Move over and I'll show you how to win this game."

And the rivalry was on. They had a fun afternoon with Kai winning the first game and Sam winning the next. They directed much teasing at both Jason and Zach for all their bragging. In their defence they answered, "We would have won if you two didn't gang up on us."

Paul and Chris served up Caesar salad and lasagne for dinner. When everyone finished their meal Chris turned out the lights and came in with a baked Alaska dessert. He set it in front of Darrel and said, "As you like to say, 'All is fair in love and war.'" He lit a cup of brandy on fire and slowly poured it over the dessert.

Darrel looked quite pleased with himself. He glanced at Sam, smiled and shrugged. "I go where my stomach leads. You're welcome to try to beat this."

Chris replied, "Yes, you can try, but I've got a lot more up my sleeve."

Zach added, "We don't mind if you want to beat Alaskan flambé."

Kai chimed in. "Yeah, we don't mind at all. In fact, I think you should make every effort to not let Chris win."

Sam looked at them all in the dim light of the fading blue flames. "Ri-i-ight. I think you guys are adding fuel to the fire for purely selfish reasons. As long as Chris and I one up each other, all you guys benefit from good eats. Don't think I'm not onto you. And as for you, Chris, enjoy this small moment." She pointed two fingers at her eyes, then at his. "I'm coming for you!"

The lads clapped and cheered, encouraging the dessert war. Chris winked at Sam. She smiled in return.

They awoke the next morning on the reefs to bright, warm sunshine. Chris and Zach set up their laptops in the dining area and started their analysis of the first week's data. Sam and Kai were busy in the wet lab with their collected samples. Before lunch Sam went to the bridge to ask Darrel if there was a possibility of taking the team diving on the reef. He gladly agreed. She spoke with Chris before making the offer over lunch. Chris and the lads were keen to take a bit of time from their afternoon to plunge into the quiet, colourful world beneath them. Maya immediately went into action. "Chris, I would really prefer for you to be my dive buddy. I'm not as experienced a diver as you and would feel more confident with you."

"Then you should buddy up with Sam. She's been diving here her whole life. She's far more experienced than I am."

"Yes, but with the possibility of sharks, I would feel safer with you."

"How about we leave the buddy pairings up to Sam. With all her diving experience, she's the dive leader."

Sam overheard the conversation. "Since you aren't very experienced, you should buddy with me for safety reasons."

Maya looked at her with clear disdain. "I'm a perfectly fine diver. Actually, it's just that I trust Chris to look out for me."

Sam asked how many times she'd been scuba diving. "Oh, I've been on over 20 dives."

"Good. We will still buddy up. And to relieve any fear, after more than two decades of diving here, I've never had a negative encounter with a shark and I've seen plenty of them. Okay, the buddies will be –"

Before she assigned them, Maya pursed her lips and turned to Chris. She held his arm and gave him a pouty smile. "I'd still feel safer if I could stay by your side."

"There's really nothing to be afraid of down there, but if staying close would make you feel better, it's fine by me."

"Good!" She handed Chris her tank and asked for his help in gearing up.

Sam caught a look shared between Zach, Kai and Jason. She was grateful they kept their thoughts to themselves. She divided the rest of them into buddies. She reviewed all the safety procedures, hand signals to be used and emergency procedures. She ran them through a predive safety check. Once done, she gave the thumbs up to go. One by one they fell backwards into the water. She never tired of this entry into another world. It felt like breaking through a portal into a completely different dimension. She loved the enveloping warmth of the Gulf waters. No matter the weather above, below remained a calm, quiet retreat.

As they checked and confirmed their gear was functioning properly, she had a moment to think. *It's funny how entering a place where my feet are no longer anchored to terra firma feels so good. Yet losing my mental and emotional footing in life feels so alarming. Maybe because hanging in place in the water wherever I want is not the same. It still offers security whereas the free falling feeling of living life without standing on Jesus, the Rock, doesn't.*

She quickly returned her attention to the dive and divers. Once she confirmed everyone was ready to go, she slowly led them down to the reef, giving plenty of time to equalize the pressure on their inner ears. She spotted a familiar manta ray gliding slowly and gracefully through the water. She turned back to the others and signalled to look. They paused their descent to hang still as the ray swam a few feet overhead. Both Kai and Zach gave the awesome signal, similar to the Hawaiian hang loose sign. She smiled – *always cool to bring people here for their first visit.*

As they wandered along the reef, she kept an eye out for the visitor favourites like turtles, hammerheads, parrotfish and eels. Even Maya seemed to be enjoying herself. As they started their ascent Sam saw what she considered the ultimate sight – a whale shark slowly swimming in the waters above. Making the whale shark signal, she directed them to look up. She watched everyone's eyes grow large. *Even marine biologists become excited about spotting one of these lone travellers.*

When they surfaced, Kai was the first to say, "Mahalo" – thanks, Hawaiian style. From their comments Sam knew they enjoyed the break from work. When they settled back to work, she noticed an improved team mood, particularly in Maya. Unfortunately she returned to her usual self by dinner.

For the following weeks the team and crew fell into a routine of collecting data along the shoreline followed by lab work while the ship patrolled the reef. Sam upped the dessert competition with peanut butter toffee cookie turtles. Chris followed up with strawberry and whipped cream crêpes. She answered with an all-out make your own sundae evening. He raised the bar with chocolate raspberry lava cakes and she trumped him with a lemon meringue torte. He came back with a mile high flourless chocolate torte. Week after week they kept the competition going, much to the delight of everyone onboard.

Several weeks after their reef dive, Sam received a phone call from Rowan. He asked how the project was going and mentioned he would be in the area for a couple of days. He hoped to have dinner with both Sam and his old colleague friend Pamela who put Sam in touch with Dr. Jay. They made arrangements to meet for dinner in Lafayette on Monday evening two weeks later. She co-ordinated with Darrel and Chris for the *Manta* to work off the coast for the first couple of days that week and to pick her up Tuesday morning.

The time passed quickly as the three month-project review meeting with NOAA officials approached. Sam and Kai collated data from the samples and experiments they'd run. They worked on a written report as well as a visual presentation to support their verbal delivery. They were both pleased at how much progress they'd made on the research. Sam was particularly satisfied with the quality of information they could contribute. She'd done enough of these projects to know their findings would significantly advance knowledge in controlling shoreline erosion.

One Thursday evening Sam and Chris sat alone together in front of the wheelhouse on the upper deck. They sat for awhile looking over the water. Sam thought she heard someone come up to the upper deck, but no one appeared.

Chris said, "Since we have the weekend ashore, would you like to come over Sunday for a ride? I suspect both King and Eddie have missed us the last couple of weeks."

"You know, I kind of miss Eddie too. Sure. What time?"

"How about you come late morning, after church? We can have lunch, then go for a long ride. And then dinner in town?"

She answered without much thought. "Okay."

"If you come to church with your family, I can drive you home afterwards."

"That's a long drive for you."

"Not really. I actually don't mind a little me time behind the wheel. It gives me the chance for some good thinking."

Before she could answer, Maya appeared. "Did I hear you say you were going riding? I'd love to come. I had such a good time when we went before."

How long has she been eavesdropping? It was probably her that I heard come up about five minutes ago. She thought about what they'd been talking about and decided it was inconsequential. *But isn't her timing interesting.*

Chris said, "Hey Maya. I only have the use of my two horses this weekend, and Sam and I started riding together before the project. Maybe you can join us another time when there is another horse available for you."

"I could double up with you. I don't mind."

"I know there's pictures of kids riding double, but I wouldn't do such a thing with adults. It is not a good idea for any horse. King looks like a strong horse, but he's built for pulling heavy loads, not carrying them on his back. He's not a motorcycle where it doesn't matter if you ride single or double. No, you'll have to wait for another time when there is a third horse available."

Predictably, Maya pouted. "I don't know anyone in town, so I'm alone all weekend. I just wanted to hang out with some friends, that's all."

"Why don't you go to Riverside Park? There are lots of trails and an amphitheatre. They always have something good on."

"Yeah, I've been there already. It's okay, I guess. What about Saturday? I could come over Saturday and you and I can go riding."

"Sorry, but I don't have any spare time this weekend. Like I said, maybe another time." Something caught Chris' eye some distance from the boat. Sam heard Maya let out a deep breath. When she looked at her, she found Maya staring back, her stare quickly turning to a glare.

Missing the exchanged looks Chris stood up. "Hey look! A pod of orcas!"

Sam came to the rail. "Yeah, it's not often you see those beauties here."

Maya looked, then huffed, turned and left.

Sam watched her leave. "I don't think she's too happy about not getting her way."

"What, Maya? No, I'm sure she's fine."

"I think you should take care in your dealings with her. Zach mentioned she has a history of isolating the top man on a project. She tried to get a professor entangled in a sexual relationship, then accused him of pressuring her into it. The university made moves to dismiss the professor, then the truth came to light. She was removed from the project and the course."

"Zach mentioned that to me, but I think she's learned her lesson and has changed. I believe she's committed to the team, our project and its success."

Sam decided to say nothing further. As long as Maya did nothing to put the project at risk, then she wouldn't inject herself between Maya and Chris.

Sunday rolled around. After church Chris brought Sam back to Des Champs de La Baie for the afternoon. When Chris threw a couple of burgers on the grill, she realized they would be dining alone.

"Where's everyone today?"

"They've flown to Kentucky to look at a new horse for Alley to start training as a replacement for Twilight when he retires." He winked. "I promise to be on my best behaviour, in case you're worried."

She laughed. "No, I'm not worried. Just wondering if I should be considering this a date."

He raised his eyebrows. "Would that be a bad thing?"

"No. But I'd like to know what to call it if someone asks."

He walked over to where she was setting the patio table. He turned her to look at him. "Hmm. Because there are hordes of people at the gate with cameras and microphones just dying to know."

She shrugged. "There could be a –"

He bent and kissed her. "I confess. I wanted some time with just you. And this was a long time in coming." He held her close and gave her a long, lingering kiss.

Sam's heart raced. She was sure her cheeks flushed red.

When he leaned back to look at her, she noticed smoke billowing from the barbeque. "Chris, the burgers!"

He ran for the barbeque and flipped the burgers. "They're a little burned."

She looked at them. "That's not burned. It's just well done."

He laughed. "That's a generously kind description. I can get another couple out of the freezer."

"No, really, it's okay. Just put a cheese slice on them and they'll be fine."

He looked at her with a smirk. "You're a distraction."

She hip checked him. "Keep up with that kind of kissing and you'll be a distraction for me too."

"Hmm. I'll take that as an open door invitation."

When they sat down to eat, he took her hand to pray over their meal and their time together.

They enjoyed a long horseback ride. As usual they finished with a cooling walk in the deeper water along the lake. They returned to the barn, hosed down and brushed the horses. He let her use the guest room shower in the house to clean up and change before going out for dinner.

He took her out to a quiet little restaurant in a historical house. The hostess led them to the beautiful garden out back and seated them under a huge oak tree with hanging Spanish moss. Candlelight flickered over a table set with white linen, crystal glassware and gold rimmed dishes.

"This is beautiful – and more than a little romantic. Have you been here before? I didn't even know this place existed."

"A buddy of mine invested in an up-and-coming chef. They opened up about a year ago. It's not exactly the kind of place you bring your mom. So no, I haven't dined here before."

"This is pretty special. I feel honoured. Thank you."

They enjoyed a leisurely dinner and a quiet walk afterward. They strolled hand in hand along Shell Beach Road, looking at the small homes built on the water, each accessed by its own dock.

They got back to the car well after dark. On the drive home he stopped for gas. While out of the car, she had a chance to think. *Things have certainly taken an unexpected turn. After leaving the country years ago because of lost love, I'm a little unsure of getting involved. I still carry the residual fear he'll connect with someone else and my love will be left trampled on the floor. The last thing I need is another failure in the relationship arena.*

She watched him head into the gas station. *We are both older and more mature now. Maybe we were too young back then to make it work. He did say he didn't want to date again unless he thought it could be something serious. He took his first kiss after suggesting a date would be okay. And he's now living his life for Christ – as*

I'm trying to do. Yes, maybe the bend in my life river has intentionally brought us back together. Oh God, is this from you? Please open this door wide so I know this is what you have given and blessed. And shut it solidly if it's not for me. I'm not really good at deciphering the path you wish me to follow, so I will need a clear closed door. I'm going to believe you've led Chris to open the door. And I will happily go along. But if you are going to shut it, I pray you do so sooner rather than later. Mom said it's not a matter of trusting people. It's a matter of trusting you. So I'm trusting you to make your will clear.

She watched him walk back toward the car. *I wonder how far back he has thought about stepping up our relationship. Pub night? The first night we went out for dinner?* Her heart danced at the memory of her day spent with the handsome man walking toward the car. The thought made her smile. *Thanks, God.*

When he dropped her off, he opened the car door for her and walked her up the steps to the front door. "I've really enjoyed today."

"Me too."

"I'd like to book all your foreseeable Sundays."

She laughed. "That's a lot of Sundays."

"It's one way of ensuring you're around in my old age to show me the photo of the old blacksmith shop."

"Oh, I see. You're just helping me out."

He smiled and let it fade. "I'd like to see you again next Sunday."

With a perky look she said, "But you see me all week."

"I'm being serious. I'd like us to start dating. You enjoyed today. Let's see where this leads."

She looked down at her fidgeting hands.

He took her hands in his. "I like you and I think you like me. We can take things slowly, if you like. We've had fun together so far. I guess I'm asking if you are interested in making it a bit more formal and calling it dating."

She thought about her gas station prayer. "Yes, I have enjoyed the time we've spent together." She paused.

"I sense there's a but coming."

"No, no. There's no but. You know I lost Andrew, my fiancé a couple of years ago. I'm now getting back into the land of the living and not letting my loss dictate my life. So I'm a little hesitant only because I'm just finding my feet." She looked up at him. "I do really like you and I like being with you." She paused, then broke into a smile. "Yes, let's give this a try."

He let out his breath. "Whew. You had me a little worried." He looked at her for a long moment, smiling. "You are very beautiful. Even more than I remembered when we were young." He pulled her in close, held her comfortably in his arms and kissed her. "So, see you tomorrow?"

"No, not tomorrow. I'm not onboard until Tuesday. I have a dinner in Lafayette tomorrow evening."

"Oh yeah. I forgot. I'll miss you."

She laughed. "I doubt it. We should talk about how to handle this onboard. I don't think it's a problem if the team finds out about us, but I think we should keep it cool while working. What do you think?"

"So no kissing while you're working in the lab?"

"I just think it'd be better for us and for the team if we keep our private life out of our work environment. It's pretty close quarters for the team to deal with a romance."

"As you wish. I won't chase you around the boat, but I'm not going to hide our relationship either. I just won't be blazingly obvious about it." He smiled. "I'm not shy to tell anyone who will listen that you're my girlfriend." He looked to the side. "My girlfriend." Smiling, he looked back at her. "It's been a long time since I've said that."

He cupped her cheek with his hand and rubbed his thumb across her lips. He gave her one more long kiss. "Goodnight, my girlfriend."

She laughed. "Goodnight, and thank you for today. I'll see you Tuesday."

He danced down the stairs. On his way to the car, he turned and blew her a kiss. She blew one back. She watched his car drive away. She put her hand on the doorknob, then paused. *Thank you, God. I'll take that as you opening the door. Please bless us as we get to know each other. Keep both of us on your path. This is quite the journey to the top of Leaving Lost – not as hard as I expected – and way more exciting.*

She took a deep breath and entered.

The next day she worked on her portion of the NOAA report from home, heading out for dinner in the late afternoon. She, Rowan and Pam had a wonderful evening together, laughing and sharing stories. She thanked the Lord on the way home for turning her life around.

10 | A Wall of Stone

The next morning Brent drove her to meet the boat at the marina in Cameron. Chris waited on the deck. When she looked at him, he winked and blew her a kiss. She laughed.

She could hear him whistling a happy tune while she worked with Kai in the lab. By noon the results from one of their experiments supported her hypothesis for the cause of decline. They would need to validate, but the results were significant enough to present to NOAA. The evidence excited both her and Kai, and the team celebrated over dinner that evening. It was her turn in the dessert competition and she brought out a black pearl mousse in a chocolate oyster shell for each person.

Chris said, "Nice! This is perfect timing with your findings today. Well played! But don't get too comfortable with your win."

Sam was satisfied with the effect of a good celebration. Even Maya stayed for dessert. She seemed unusually pleasant to everyone for a change.

The following day while a storm blew in, they worked along the shores of Vermilion Bay. Sam and Kai collected more samples for additional experiments and Zach, Maya and Chris gathered data from the eroding shoreline. Over the afternoon the winds had picked up. Along with a full moon and a building high tide, the waves were unusually rough, making for a rocky night.

The next morning Sam was surprised to find they were pulling into Cameron marina. She spotted both Dr. Jay and Dr. Finstedt on the dock, awaiting their arrival. Chris came on deck with the others.

Chris asked, "Wonder what's going on. Have you talked with Darrel?"

"No. I don't know what's up. They look rather serious."

Once the boat was tied up, the two men boarded and Dr. Finstedt asked to speak with Sam privately. Dr Jay and the others went inside, leaving them alone.

"I'll get right to the point, Samantha. I don't know what you've become used to in Scotland, but here at NOAA we don't accept unethical behaviour by employees or contracted team members."

Sam paled. She felt queasy. "I have no idea what you're talking about, but I assure you I've done nothing unethical."

He looked hard at her. His face turned red. "Okay. If you insist on dragging out the dirty laundry, I received this email from you Monday, I assume by mistake. You clearly ask a real estate agent to purchase several tracts of land along the Pecan Island coast through a holding company. Currently the land is worth little because of the severe erosion. With a successful project this land would double or triple in value. I checked. You attended our ethics course, so you surely know this is a violation of our policies. That alone is enough to remove you from the project, and you can be assured you will never work for NOAA or the university again.

"But what angers me personally is how you suggest we are too stupid to catch on to you. I am appalled. You've covered yourself in shameful behaviour and you've stained all those who recommended you." He handed her an envelope.

With shaking hands she accepted it and pulled out the paperwork. "You will find a notice of dismissal and a termination of our contract with you. Now, I will go with you to your quarters. You can gather your things and I'll escort you off the ship."

She stared blankly at the paper. "But I don't understand. I never sent you any email. And I'm not purchasing any property. This is all a big mistake."

"That's what I thought at first, but we have confirmed this came from the computer assigned to you and have verified you were the one logged in at the time. If you wish any further conversation, you can do so through our lawyers. Their contact information is included in your dismissal letter. Now, get your things. I'll discuss this no further."

As they headed toward her quarters, she saw Dr. Jay leaving with her computer. She gathered her personal belongings and started for the deck. On her way past the mess, she caught Darrel's eye. He looked at her with concern then looked down.

Dr. Jay waited on the dock. Sam said, "Honestly, I have no idea what this is about. I didn't send that email and I certainly didn't purchase any property."

He slowly shook his head. "The evidence is very clear. We checked with the real estate agent and he confirmed you've put in offers on several pieces of land."

Dr. Finstedt added, "I'm shocked and very disappointed. You certainly put on a good front. You had me fooled."

Once they stepped off the boat, the men watched for a moment as it pulled away.

She turned to them. "I don't blame you. I understand you think the evidence is damning. But I did *not* do this. I would like the chance to clear my name."

Dr. Finstedt answered, "As I said, any further dealings will be with our lawyers." They turned and left her standing alone on the dock. She watched as they drove away. She turned and watched the *Manta* disappearing past Monkey Island. Finally she read the papers. The letter stated they would be forwarding the issue to the Department of Justice (DOJ) to determine if she had violated the law and to what extent. She swallowed, but her mouth had gone dry. *This is unbelievable. I haven't done any of this, yet they are talking about taking me to court. This is pretty serious. I think I need a lawyer – a really good one.* She read further. *I'm not to contact the team or crew?*

She called home to get Brent to pick her up. Once home she told everyone what happened and showed each of them the two documents. "Just so we're all clear on this, I didn't do what they said."

Jessie rubbed her daughter's back. "I know, honey."

Brent said, "You're going to need a lawyer. Let me call Frank from church. He will know of someone who is experienced in this area and can help out." He left to make the call.

"Oh Mom. What am I going to do? This could mean the end of any work in my field." Tears flowed as she caught her breath. "I'm scared. I thought things were going so well, you know? I was determined to walk God's path and everything seemed to be coming together. Now it's all exploded. There is nothing good about any of this."

Her mom quietly listened.

"None of this is fair. They didn't even give me the chance to explain my side. They had their supposed evidence and they've decided I'm guilty. I thought with God on my side, stuff like this wouldn't happen. How can God let this happen? I'm doing my best to be a good Christian. How can this be called living under the shelter of His wings? This isn't a rock on my path. This is a solid rock wall that's falling on top of me. I'm going to be flattened."

As she drew her breath, her mom reached for her hand. "My sweet girl. I know this looks really bad. But you are in the middle of one of life's storms. Of all times, this is not the time to walk away from God. He did not bring this on you. Oh, He knew it was on your path and I can assure you He knows the way to overcome. Now, of all times, is the time to lean on Him."

"It's not easy, Mom. This means my reputation and could mean my career."

"If a stone is worth standing on and if it's big enough to develop your faith, then you can't expect it to be all easy. Remember my journal of stones? I've written about the hard times of life. They aren't about times when I stood on top of the mountain and life was easy. Nor are they about times when everything was going my way. Any difficult time in life that disappears without ever having a fiery trial is a stone that will crumble under your feet when you go to stand in faith on it. You are building a stone of faith you can stand on – a stone you can look back on and say, 'There is evidence that God will take me through any crisis.'

"By no means am I saying this will be easy. It's scary – really scary. But God specializes in using the huge storms, those impossible situations, to do His most amazing work. When I see a big thing on my path, like this or like cancer, I know to hold on tight and watch with anticipation as He does the impossible, the unimaginable, the inconceivable."

"I know that's how you see it, but I don't have that kind of faith. I'm angry at the injustice and I'm scared for my future."

"I know. That is how the human part of you wants to react. But we are a new creature. The old is gone and the new is here. We no longer live by flesh, but by our spirit. That old nature of anger and fear was nailed to the cross. We've been raised up to walk in the newness of our spiritual life. So now is the time to ask Him to strengthen you, the new creature – to ask to see this situation as He sees it. You need to open your spiritual eyes." She paused. "How about we pray together?"

She wiped away the rolling tears from her face, sniffed and nodded.

"Dear heavenly Father, thank you for caring for us as your own children. Thank you for engraving Sam's name on your hand, for having her in front of your mind. You know the beginning and the end, and all things in-between. You know all that has happened to bring Sam to this place. You know the truth of what happened. Today we ask that you would give

Sam the spiritual strength to see this from a heavenly perspective. Fill her with your courage. Give her heavenly peace that all of this rests in your hands, and fill her heart with the confidence that she can reliably wait on your provision in the face of the impossible.

"We pray for your intervention in this situation. We are your children and bear your great name. We ask that you would give us your wisdom to say and do what you would have us do. Help Sam to live by the spirit and not by the flesh. And we thank you in advance for guiding us through the storm and bringing us through to the other side stronger in you. In the sweet name of Jesus we pray, amen.

"Thanks, Mom."

She kissed her daughter's head. "I love you very much, you know."

Brent came back from talking on the phone. "I've got the name of a guy in Houston. He has a great reputation in dealing with wrongful dismissals. He'll call you this afternoon. In the meantime Frank suggested we scan all the paperwork and email it to this guy. And when you get an appointment, I'd be happy to go with you, if you want."

She stood up and gave him a hug. "Thanks, Dad. She kissed his cheek and smiled. "Maybe I'm not too old to have my daddy go with me."

"If you'd prefer to go alone, that's fine too."

"No, Dad. I'd be enormously grateful to have you there. I think you bring your experience and wisdom. And I'd be glad to lean on your strength."

"Okay, Chickadee. You and me it is."

The phone rang and she thought it might be the lawyer, but it was for Kyle. He came back to tell them he was assigned to an emergency project in Virginia and needed to leave immediately. He packed and hugged his mom and dad goodbye. He took Sam's hand. "I know God will work out this mess. I'll keep praying for you. Keep me posted on how things go with the lawyer."

She spoke with Jonah Silverman in the afternoon and made arrangements to meet with him the following afternoon. The next day they arrived a few minutes early to Jonah's well-appointed office. Sam took one look and said, "Oh Dad, I can't afford this kind of lawyer."

"You can't afford anything less."

She took a deep breath and sat down. Promptly they were called into Jonah's office. He was an older, stout gentleman in Texas attire. He greeted them and offered a couple of leather chairs.

"Well, shall we get right down to business?" He opened a file folder. "I received your emailed documents. Thank you for sending those. We've been in touch with the lawyers from NOAA and the DOJ, and requested the name of the real estate agent and the holding company you are allegedly using to purchase property. As well, we requested a copy of the email they claim you sent accidentally to Dr. Finstedt. They've sent us everything we requested. This morning I put one of our investigators on the trail of this land purchase."

"Mr. Silverman, it seems a big expense to have an investigator. Are you sure that's necessary?"

"Call me Jonah, please. I'm not sure if you fully realize the gravity of your situation. If we cannot prove you have nothing to do with these land purchases, they can criminally charge you with statute 18 of the U.S. code section 208." He noted her pale face. "So while this is serious and we must proceed with this investigation, let's not get ahead of ourselves. Tell me your side of the story."

"There isn't really any story on my side. Yesterday both Dr. Finstedt and Dr. Jay met the boat at the marina and gave me the documents you have, escorted me off the boat and left me standing on the dock. Dr. Finstedt said they verified the message came from my computer and my login. And Dr. Jay said they confirmed the real estate agent and the holding company. They refused to discuss it any further with me. They just directed me to their lawyers. And it says I'm not to contact any member of the team."

"Yes. I know this is hard, but it is really important that you don't contact the team. Leave all correspondence to us. Now, do you know Ms. Tuesday Revere?"

"Tuesday Revere? No, I don't know anyone named Tuesday. It doesn't even sound like a real name. "

"Indeed. Nonetheless, there is a real estate agent named Tuesday Revere. Okay, do you possess any land trusts? Or have you ever purchased land by way of a trustee?

"No."

"While it can be difficult to identify the real owner in a land trust, we have a couple of avenues we can pursue to expose this information. It may take us a week or two to do so. In the meantime, you need to hold tight. We will resolve this for you. Provided you are not involved, we should be able to prove so and thus prevent criminal charges."

Brent asked, "What is the possibility that you won't be able to uncover the real names of the people involved?"

"If there have been purchases, we are generally able to get to the names. If they have yet to make a purchase, then there is no criminal action and the government has no grounds by which to charge you."

Sam blurted, "I don't want to just not be charged! I want my name cleared of any involvement in this! I want the proof this is someone else!"

"I know this can be very difficult to accept, but if there has been no purchased land, there will be no evidence. Is there anyone who would like to frame you? Anyone with a grudge against you?"

"No. I don't do anything that would cause someone to do this. Setting me up for criminal charges is pretty extreme. I'm just a scientist. I lead a very quiet life studying invertebrates."

"Have you or are you working on any research that will prove profitable?"

"No. Whatever we find will be made freely available to the State and landowners. Honestly, I can't think of any reason why someone would do this, let alone who. And yet, here we are."

"Good. Well, we will get to the bottom of it." He made a few notes on his pad.

Brent asked, "Jonah, should we be worried about someone trying to physically harm Sam?"

"This kind of thing and violence don't usually go hand in hand unless it's organized crime. Nonetheless, it wouldn't hurt to be more cautious until we resolve the matter."

Jonah stood up. "Give us a week or two. We will be in touch as soon as we know something concrete, but if you're worried, feel free to call my assistant and she can update you. Again, don't worry. We'll work to get this sorted out in a few weeks."

On their drive home Sam tried to sort out who would be targeting her. Once home they told Jessie what Jonah had said. They all agreed. She should not go to the reef at all in case they ran into the *Manta*, and she shouldn't take a dive group out alone.

While helping her mom in the kitchen, she said, "It seems that just when I decided to walk closer to God, this nightmare starts. I don't know if I have the strength to not be afraid. Quite honestly, I feel sick-to-my-stomach scared."

"Life can dish out some pretty difficult situations. Some we cannot see any good coming at the end, but I know I'd rather go through something like this in God's care than trying to go it alone. You are going to have to go through the storm. The only question is whether you choose to go it alone or follow God's leading to His good thing. Remember, He works out all things for good for those who are His own. It is in our worst storms that His very presence can quell the devastating winds."

"So, what you're saying is now is not the time to bail."

"Yes, and more. If you shelter under the wing of God, then not only can you be assured of a good outcome, but you can also be assured of the quiet peace that surpasses all understanding during the storm. He tells us to lay out our problems before Him, and then thank Him for looking after us. And He will fill you with peace about the whole situation."

After dinner she went to the boathouse and sat on the WaveRunner. She prayed about all her fears – about someone hating her that much, about losing her job, losing her reputation, her career.

It is so hard to not be afraid. I really need you now. I need your comforting presence and I am going to lean on your promise of filling me with your peace. I don't really know how to overcome my fears and I need your help.

She paused, watching a container ship in the distance. *What does the Bible say about that peace? Guard your hearts and minds by thinking about things that are pure, and lovely, and admirable, things that are excellent and worthy of praise.*

Her mind turned to Chris. *My budding relationship with him was something that was becoming good and lovely. Oh God, I was so sure you were opening the door for us. But now he's going to think I'm a criminal. He's not going to want anything to do with me.* Tears formed in her eyes. *I just wasn't prepared for another loss. I hadn't realized how far I'd let my heart go and now I regret it. Lord, did I misinterpret something as an open door that really wasn't? This is a mess and I'm a mess. I really need your peace about all of it.*

She saw a heron walking toward her along the shoreline. In the late afternoon sunlight he held out his wing to cast a shadow on the water to see the fish. She watched its slow deliberate steps, its cocked head and concentration. It struck its beak into the water with lightning speed and speared a fish.

Well done! When the heron flew off, she realized she'd spent the time watching it, free of fear. *Right. Think about things that are worthy of praise. Look at God's creation and know if He cares for His creatures, how much more He's involved in my life.* She leaned back on the seat, closed her eyes and spent some time praising God for all He had and was doing in her life. When she returned to the house, she felt free of the consuming fear. *Now I need to stay on top of my thoughts and not allow the negative back in.*

That evening she lay in bed thinking about how her week started with joy and hope always found in a new relationship, and how things had spun to desperate in a moment. *Okay Lord, I see that this is a giant crevice in my Leaving Lost stone. I know you are teaching me to follow your ways of prayer, thanksgiving and thinking on all that is good. Like King David suggested, even though I walk through the darkest valley, your rod of comfort and staff of support – the tools you use to guide and defend your own – remove my fears. Your word and your spirit comfort me.*

Thank you for guiding me through this chasm. I look forward to the view from the top of Leaving Lost and to the day I can truly say, "I've come through and now stand in faith on this stone."

Leaving Lost

11 | A Stinking Container

Without work Sam had plenty of time to think. Each day seemed endless. Hours crawled by. Staying focused on the good things of the Lord proved a challenge. Almost by the minute she caught her mind wandering to the worst case scenario of becoming a convicted criminal. *What if Jonah and his detectives can't uncover the truth? What if I never find out who's behind this? What if I can't prove my innocence and end up in jail?*

She read comforting words in Isaiah 26:3– "You will keep in perfect peace all who trust in you, all whose thoughts are fixed on you!" *That's great. The problem is that I can't seem to keep my mind fixed on you. God, I really need help. This is the most difficult thing I've ever had to deal with.*

She read on through Isaiah and found verse 17 in chapter 54 that reached through her anxiety. "No weapon turned against you will succeed. You will silence every voice raised up to accuse you. These benefits are enjoyed by the servants of the Lord; their vindication will come from me. I, the Lord, have spoken!"

She then searched the Internet and found some interesting verses in 2 Corinthians 4:8–9 that she really felt spoke to her situation. "We are pressed on every side by troubles, but we are not crushed. We are perplexed, but not driven to despair. We are hunted down, but never abandoned by God. We get knocked down, but we are not destroyed."

While floating in the pool that afternoon, she looked to the sky. *I do feel pressed in and hunted, but you promise I will not be driven to despair and you will not abandon me. And you promised no evil plot formed against me will succeed and that I will silence this voice that accuses me. You confirmed this promise as one you spoke into the record. Okay, in my head I understand you have promised it, and have permanently recorded your promise for me this day. But to be really honest, I still see no way out of this mess. And I see no good coming from this accusation. I'm scared and I don't have the strength to remove myself from my fears. They have a deep hold on me. I am tangled in their tentacles. I really need you, God, to step in and help me. I really can't do this on my own. I can't even keep my mind on you, but I keep looking at the storm, at the hurricane winds, rain and hail threatening to wipe me out. It seems so dark and hopeless. I don't see you anywhere. You promised to strengthen me and help me. Well, today is the day I need all you offer.*

She started to cry, not of self-pity, but because she felt a loving warmth fill her heart and knew this was evidence of the Lord. He was revealing Himself in a tangible way for her, to bolster her and let her know she was not alone. She drew in a deep breath and thanked Him for His presence and reassurance. *This is all in your hands. There is nothing I can do to resolve this. Please give the detective the wisdom to find the person behind this attack and uncover the evidence to prove me innocent. Thank you, Jesus, for your comforting presence. Please don't leave me. In your name I pray, amen.*

When Sunday rolled around, she decided not to go to church with her family, as she didn't want to run into Chris and then be accused of contacting someone from the team. It proved pointless as Chris, nor anyone from his family, were there. She half expected him to reach out to her by the weekend, but as the days passed with no call or email, Sam concluded he wanted nothing more to do with her. She understood. *Why would he want anything to do with a person about to be convicted?*

By Sunday evening she told the Lord how disappointed she felt and how it hurt to have Chris walk in and out of her life for the second time. As soon as she shared her feelings, she felt the Lord correcting her.

Yes, you're right. He didn't officially walk out last time. And I don't have proof he's walked out this time either. But still, I am feeling a bit abandoned.

She paused to listen to the quiet voice of the Lord whispering to her mind and heart. "I have my promise written down for you. I have vowed to never leave you or abandon you. I know you are weak. You can lean entirely on me. In me you will find the strength and courage to face the storms of life. You do not stand alone. I know the end and I have already prepared a way for you. I will shelter you day and night while the storm rages. Remember, I made you, I created you with a need for me because I am the one who will carry you through life."

She remembered her mother's words of advice. *No matter how good a man is, he cannot be my rock. Only God is the Prince Charming who can meet all my needs. She pondered God's promise of working all things out for good. I understand this to be true, but I am so weak that I can't even stand on that promise without doubting. I look at my circumstances and let the reality of my situation draw my eyes and my faith away from you. I quickly become mired in fear and feelings of abandonment. Oh God, forgive me for my lack of faith. How can I know your promises and know you cannot lie, yet doubt you will deliver on your promises for me? What kind of feeble-minded person am I?"*

"I have promised in your weakness I am strong. I will help you even in your weakness. Draw in close. Take all that fear and worry, all your feelings of abandonment, and turn them over to me. And when you give them to me, I then can replace them with my peace."

She thought for a long moment. Then she went to the kitchen to find a jar. Unable to find one she settled on a plastic container with a locking lid. She grabbed a permanent marker along with the keys to the WaveRunner. She steered south to an area of mudflats she knew to be particularly putrid. In her bare feet she walked out and scooped up some mud to fill the plastic container. She locked down the lid on all four sides and set it on the footrest as she pushed the WaveRunner back into the water. After rinsing off she headed back home.

Once in her room she knelt down. On one side of the container she wrote the word fear. On the next side she wrote abandoned. One the third side, doubt. And on the fourth side, weak. *Okay God. This holds my failings. I know they are stinky and foul, but that's me today. Now I want to give it all to you. Please take this stinking mess from me and replace it with your peace that is beyond comprehension. You promised to be my strength. Today, right now, I turn this all over to you. Thank you that not only do you promise to make a way through life's storm, but you also give me all I need in my weakness to help me hang on to your promises. In your name Jesus – the name that holds all power – I pray, amen.*

Immediately she felt a release – a calm. For several minutes she thanked God for helping clean out the negative and filling her with Himself. She set the container on her dresser so she could see it whenever she was in her room and remember she'd turned it all over to God, and in exchange He'd filled her with rest. Over the next days she returned to look at it whenever negative feelings pressed in. She'd speak to the conflicting thoughts and remind them they had been given to God and replaced. Having a symbolic but tangible representation helped keep her focused on the work God completed inside her.

12 | In the Midst of a Crevice

Almost two weeks after meeting with Jonah, he called. Anxiously Sam got through the standard small talk. "I'm fine, thanks. So, what is the news? Have you figured out who is behind this?"

"No, not yet, but my detective is making good progress and remains confident he will uncover the truth. What I'm calling about is the DOJ lawyers have informed me they will be pressing charges against you. You should receive notification in the next day or two. The court documents will confirm the charges, the court date, time and location. It's scheduled for two weeks from today in New Orleans."

"Oh, wow! You'll be there, right?"

"Yes. I'll be handling this personally. We'll talk before then and if this does go ahead, we'll meet a couple of hours beforehand to go through the case and talk about what you can expect."

"Do you think the detective will be successful by then? What if he hasn't found evidence that I didn't do this?"

"We still have two weeks. He's the best of the best. But I do need to be frank. If he doesn't dig up evidence, their case against you is significant. We can pull in character witnesses, but as I'm sure you already know, they do not carry the same weight as their evidence.

"As I said, we have two weeks and Bill is making good progress. I spoke with him yesterday and he said he is confident he will get to the truth. So let's not worry just yet."

"You'll let me know as soon as you have anything, right?"

"Absolutely. Bill knows how anxious we are to resolve this and will contact me as soon as he has something."

"Okay. Thanks."

"Take care and don't hesitate to call if you have any concerns."

She immediately went to her room to look at the mud-filled container. She turned it around, reading the words – fear, abandoned, doubt and weak. She knelt beside her bed, holding it up in her hands. *Oh God, the negative is pressing in again and I'm too weak on my own to push it out. You promised in your Word that if I bring my needs to you, leave them with you and think on your good things you will fill me with your abundant peace. I have a bunch of new worries – even darker and more burdensome. You are my Lord and Saviour. I need to shelter under your protective wing. Wash the thick mud of fear out of my heart and mind. I give you this container, now filled with my fear. Take it from me and fill me with your thoughts – thoughts of all that is good. Let me see your goodness. Let me see the light at the end of this dark valley.* She drew in a breath and held it for a moment. Letting it out she imagined releasing all the negative thoughts and feelings.

Feeling the warm presence of God, she put the container back on the dresser and spent the rest of the day with her parents around the pool.

The days passed slowly, each one required Sam to push back on the incessant fear and doubt. At first it seemed to be winning, but she managed to get to the place where she conquered it and she enjoyed the Lord's peace. She kept reminding herself that God promised to work this all out for her good.

She woke up every day hoping it would be the one with good news from the detective. But day upon day passed with nothing. She spoke with Jonah several times and they made arrangements for people to testify on her behalf. When the day of the court proceedings arrived, she accepted this was the road God had for her to walk. She'd prayed about strength for the day and knew the Lord was right beside her.

The bank of lawyers from the DOJ laid out their evidence. Even she had to admit it looked damning. When the lead lawyer stood to turn the court over to the defence, Dr. Jay, Chris and another man hurriedly entered the court and spoke to the DOJ lawyers. The lead lawyer asked for and was granted a ten-minute recess.

Sam asked Jonah what was going on. "It looks like they have new evidence."

She watched closely, straining to hear what they were saying. Dr. Jay handed over several documents and the three men bent down talking over each other to explain what they'd found. As the third man sat down to answer questions, Chris stood up and looked over at Sam for the first time. He smiled and winked at her, and mouthed, "It's going to be okay."

She smiled back at Chris. "Thank you."

The DOJ lawyers called Jonah over to discuss the new evidence.

Brent leaned forward and held her hand.

When the judge returned, Jonah returned, and the three men took a seat behind the DOJ lawyers.

Sam whispered, "What's going on?"

Jonah smiled. "Don't worry. This is good news."

Before he could tell her anything more, the lead DOJ lawyer stood up. "Your Honour. We have new evidence, irrefutable evidence that Samantha Morgan did not send the email and was not involved in purchasing property. We now ask the court to dismiss this case against Miss Morgan as we will be pursuing charges of fraud against another person."

The judge turned to Jonah. He stood up. "Your Honour, we would request that the prosecution pays for all defence costs associated with this case."

"Agreed. Submit your client's costs to the court. NOAA and the DOJ will be responsible for reimbursing the costs fully. Case dismissed."

The judge dismissed the courtroom. Sam heaved a deep sigh of relief. The lead lawyer came to talk with Jonah and Sam. Chris and Dr. Jay joined him.

"Miss Morgan, please accept my apologies. These three men have just brought evidence of your innocence. We will be pursuing several charges against Maya Treadwell." He shook their hands and left.

Dr. Jay said, "Sam, I am truly sorry this all has happened. Please accept my apologies on behalf of NOAA. I've talked with Dr. Finstedt and while I understand if you say no, we'd like you to consider coming back on the project. We had no idea Maya could be so vengeful and we profusely apologize for exposing you to her wrath. You have proven yourself principled and honest. We would be more than honoured to have you return. If you cannot see your way clear to do so, I would be glad to write you a letter of my highest recommendations, and if you would let me, I will offer my support in helping you find other work. Again, I cannot fully express my deep regret over what we've put you through."

Tears sprang to Sam's eyes. She hardly knew what to say.

"Please don't feel you need to give me an answer today. Call me if you want to talk." He nodded to Jonah and her father, and left.

Chris stepped in close and opened his arms. She leaned in and hugged him. "I thought you'd lost interest in me when it looked like I was a criminal."

"You're no criminal. I never believed you'd done any of this and I never lost interest in you. I didn't want to risk any contact with you until things were resolved in case it put you in jeopardy. You need to know that no one on the boat believed you to be a criminal. We all worked to figure out what actually happened. Well, all of us except Maya. She kept talking about what a horrible person you must be. And that got us thinking that maybe she was involved. When we found out what they'd accused you of, we realized you weren't even onboard when that email was sent from your computer. So we got Joey from the IT department to find evidence the email was sent from your laptop onboard the ship, not just through web-mail, and that it happened while you were in Lafayette. That is part of the evidence we gave to the lawyers. It is solid evidence that it wasn't you.

"Dr. Jay and Dr. Finstedt along with one of their lawyers interviewed Maya with this evidence in hand. At first she denied she was connected with this, but we had evidence from her own computer login that she was in regular correspondence with the real estate agent involved in the land purchases. That cracked her and she finally admitted she'd set you up. She was immediately dismissed from the project. I suspect she will end up in jail for this one. I was so wrong about her and you were so right. I'm sorry I didn't listen to you.

"Just know the team and the crew would all love to have you back on the project. I'd be particularly happy if you would come back. Either way, I'd like us to get back to spending time together."

Sam invited Chris to drive back with her and her father. She called her mom to give her the good news once they were in the car and they thanked the Lord for His intervention.

They stopped at a restaurant to eat before the long drive home. She excused herself to go to the bathroom. She wanted a few moments alone to thank her Lord for intervening. *I can see the road through now and I can see how you've worked this all out for me. I couldn't see how it was going to work out, but you were faithful and delivered me. Thank you for guiding my behaviour and keeping me on your path. For Dr. Jay to say I'm honourable and honest is because of you keeping me steady on your path. Thank you for preserving, even enhancing my reputation. Oh, and thank you for the return of Chris as well. I see now you preserved that relationship through all this. Indeed, Chris is a door you have opened for me and you have kept open. I can't say thank you enough. This was a deep, dark crevice in the Leaving Lost rock and you have brought me through.*

Leaving Lost

13 | Crowns of Praise

No one asked Sam if she intended to return to NOAA. She knew every-one would understand should she decide to move on. In fact, most would expect it might be too awkward to continue with the project. The day after the court case dismissal she joined her father on his boat. He was doing some general maintenance.

She asked him what he thought about whether she should contin-ue with the project. "My Chickadee, that decision is all yours. You loved the project work, the team, the crew and Dr. Jay. On the other hand, if it would be uncomfortable for you, then you have the option of moving on. No one will think any less of you. It sounds like NOAA will support you either way."

"What would you do if you were me?"

"Before I answer that, what do you want to do?"

"I really want to continue with the project, but I don't know if it will be too awkward."

"For who?"

"Well, it might be a bit awkward for me at first. But I guess I'm most worried about what it will be like with Dr. Finstedt and Dr. Jay. I wonder if we can get back to the relationship we had before without them trying to compensate for their error in judgement. I just want to be treated fairly."

"Then I think you should continue. I think you can find a way to put everyone at ease. If you make it clear at the beginning that you expect to be treated fairly, not with kid gloves, then I think you'll set the tone and everyone will fall in line."

"So – what would you do if you were me?'"

He smiled. "I think either road is a good choice. Continuing with the project is definitely the high road. I suspect it is the road Jesus would choose, but it could be a more difficult one. Not everyone is cut out for that road. I admire you for wanting to continue with your commitment to the project. And I think you bring with you a lot of respect. You have an opportunity to earn even more respect by fulfilling your role and expecting no particular favour. And I know the Lord will continue to walk with you and bring favour onto your path." He stopped working and looked at her. "My little chickadee has grown up into a fantastic woman I'm so very proud of."

"Thanks, Dad. I feel good about the decision. And I'm glad you are proud of me."

She called Dr. Jay and asked if he would meet her for lunch the next day.

She got to the restaurant ahead of him. When he arrived she stood up and shook his hand, thanking him for coming. They got through some stilted small talk and ordered their meals. When the waitress left, she said, "I wanted to talk to you about coming back to the project."

"We would all like you back."

"I have a bit of hesitation because I'm concerned people might feel awkward. I would like everything to return to the way it was. I don't want any special treatment. I just want to be treated fairly. I know you offered to give me a letter of the highest recommendation right now. I'd like that letter when the project is complete and I've *earned* your commendations for my work."

His eyebrows rose. Then he looked down at the table and shook his head. She was beginning to feel nervous. He finally looked up at her. "You are a very remarkable woman. We would be very honoured to have you back on the team. I think it's impressive that you don't want to take advantage of the situation. The more I know you, the more I find I admire you."

Smiling he said, "You are indeed wise. Yes, I might have tended to make it up to you through favouring you. If I try my best to not let your grace affect me too much, will you return?"

She laughed at his use of the word try. "You promise you will legitimately try?"

He paused.

She said, "Listen, I respect you and the knowledge you bring to the project. I would like to think you are prepared to still lead the team and if I wander away from the direction you intend, you're going to continue to hold the reins of leadership. I want our working relationship to carry forward as though none of this happened."

"Okay. I promise to lead the team as I would have had this never happened. But I cannot lessen my admiration and respect for you as a person and a colleague. I don't know too many people who would have conducted themselves with your grace and strength. Also, I've spent some time with Kai going through your work to date and I must say, you have done a fantastic job with the research and with team leadership. Yes, I've heard all about your dessert war with Chris. Even my crew speaks very highly of you. I think you would agree if you had someone working under you doing such a great job, you would give her quite a bit of leeway to do her work. You've proven through your work you are worthy of my favour. So I would argue I can effectively manage the team and still let you be my favourite scientist."

She laughed and had a hint of a blush. "Thank you, Dr. Jay. I appreciate you sharing your thoughts on my work as that makes me feel more comfortable about coming back. I just don't want anyone to say I wasn't held to your standard."

"Not to worry. There is plenty of evidence in your work to warrant a boss' favour. And I'll be glad to straighten out anyone who says otherwise." He bowed his head slightly and looked up at her through his eyebrows. "So, want to start tomorrow?"

She thought about how easily they spoke honestly with each other and how she felt comfortable with him. She smiled brightly. "Yes!"

They enjoyed a light and easy meal discussing her work on the project and what had been done in her absence. He mentioned Kai had filled in for her, and while he felt he had done as well as could be expected, his inexperience had slowed the research progress and showed in his first report to NOAA.

When they parted, Dr. Jay said he'd meet her at the docks the next morning and join them onboard for a few days. And he thanked her again for rejoining the project.

She drove home satisfied with her decision. With a thankful heart she called Chris onboard the *Manta* to excitedly talk over the dramatic changes that occurred over the last couple of days with Jesus. That evening the family celebrated.

The next morning when Brent dropped her off at the docks, she saw both Dr. Jay and Dr. Finstedt waiting for her. There was no sign of the *Manta*. She wondered if Dr. Finstedt cancelled the offer to rejoin the team. "Dad, would you mind waiting a few minutes? I'll wave if I don't need a ride back home."

"I'll pray for favour and wisdom. Know that the Lord walks with you."

"Thanks, Dad."

As she walked toward the dock the two men met her halfway. "Hi,

Dr. Jay." She offered her hand to Dr. Finstedt. "Hi, Dr. Finstedt."

He shook her hand. "I wanted to join Dr. Jay in meeting you this morning. Let me first offer my apologies. You have impressed an old man and I thought I was beyond being impressed. I saw the email evidence, but failed to look at the person. There was plenty to see in your work and your relations for me to understand who you are, but I let the email anger me and cloud my assessment. Will you forgive my error in judgement? Will you forgive me and forgive all I said to you?"

She turned back to her dad and waved, indicating he could leave. Looking back at Dr. Finstedt, she could feel threatening tears. "Oh, you are going to make me cry and I've never done that in front of my boss or my boss' boss. Yes, I forgive you. I'm sure Dr. Jay spoke with you about our conversation yesterday. I'd like to reiterate to you that I want to go back to the working relationship we had before all this happened."

"Yes, Jay and I did talk about you yesterday. I have a favourite quote from Oliver Wendell Holmes. I usually use it in an academic situation, but I think it fits quite well here. 'Man's mind, once stretched by a new idea, never regains its original dimensions.' My dear, this experience has stretched my concept of you. You and I can never go back to the relationship we had before. And I do not wish to dismiss my new view of you. You must accept that time and events mould our impression of others. And I admire and respect you. Even more so now that you are graciously returning to the project with a humble spirit. I will tell you now that you will always have work with NOAA for as long as you want. Thank you for respecting and forgiving a mistaken old man."

"Oh Dr. Finstedt. Thank you for such kind words."

"I don't say this to everyone, but please, call me Charles."

"How about Dr. Charles?"

He nodded in agreement, then took her hand and patted it. "Thank *you* for forgiving me. And thank you for your work. Jay has informed me of the quality of your research and the progress you've made." He looked around. "Now, where is the *Manta*?"

Dr. Jay answered, "I just got a text from Darrel. He said to expect them in a couple of minutes."

They looked out toward the Gulf and saw the *Manta* rounding the point of land. They laughed. Hanging from the bow was a big sign – "We missed you, Sam." The team and crew were all on the upper deck waving wildly at them. She waved back equally. She and Dr. Jay caught the ropes to tie off while they boarded and loaded both her gear and the mysterious boxes of Dr. Jay's.

Each person welcomed her warmly. She was relieved there was no hesitation or stiffness. Kai said, "I'm so glad you're back. I tried, but I cannot fill your shoes."

"Thank you, Kai. And I appreciate the work you've done to keep the project moving forward. I hear from Dr. Jay you've done well. You'll need to catch me up on all you've done. And then we'll need to get busy so we're ready for the next update."

Kai said, "Welina. Ho'oponopono."

"I know welina is a warm greeting, but I don't know ho'oponopono."

"It means things have been set right or rectified."

She held Kai's hand for a brief moment. "Welina."

After she'd greeted everyone Dr. Finstedt said, "I wanted to say a few things to everyone before I leave you folks to get on your way. First, I was very wrong about Sam and she's graciously forgiven me. I'd like everyone to know that Dr. Jay, NOAA and especially me – we really appreciate Sam's commendable conduct. She has indeed walked the high road and shown herself to be a model of ethics and comportment despite my mistaken assessment of her. As well, her work on this project has been stellar. In everything she has proven herself above reproach. She's graciously agreed to continue working for NOAA. I think I speak for Jay and myself. Sam has earned our admiration and respect. Also, I would like to thank the rest of the team, and in particular Kai for carrying on with the project in the interim.

"And one final piece of news for all of you. Maya's father said he apologizes for his daughter's behaviour. He had no idea she was so out of control. He did offer to double his bonus to the project. He knows this doesn't make up for the damage Maya has done, but wanted us and Sam in particular to know he's sorry."

Sam nodded her acceptance. He finished by saying, "Now, I will leave you folks to your work." He winked at Darrel. "Enjoy your evening celebration on me."

Sam smiled. "Thank you so much, Dr. Charles."

"Take care, my dear."

She nodded.

He pulled Chris to the side for a quiet word, and then stepped back onto the dock. He threw the tie ropes onto the boat, gave them a push out and waved goodbye.

Chris asked, "Well now, team meeting in the mess?"

They all headed in. On the table was a giant 3 ft. chocolate chip cookie. Chris smiled. "I thought we could use a little snack as we catch up on the project."

They quickly fell into comfortable ease with each other. The conversation moved onto the details of the project. They spent the morning resetting their plan to accommodate the lost momentum and catching her up on the findings in both streams of work.

In the early afternoon Dr. Jay, Sam and Chris discussed the money donated by Maya's father in the wheelhouse with Darrel. They agreed to add a phase 2 to the project involving Chris and Sam to work with NOAA personnel, State and parish workers to implement their findings in phase 1.

Dr. Jay and Darrel worked in the kitchen for the remainder of the afternoon. They banned all visitors while they prepared the evening meal. When they called everyone to dinner, the mess was done up in helium balloons and streamers. Inspired by all things Cajun, they enjoyed a big meal of crawfish, jambalaya, creole chicken, gumbo, dirty rice and blackened catfish. For dessert they served a couple of Southern Comfort ice cream pies with candles for Sam to blow out. She now understood what was in all of Dr. Jay's mystery boxes.

That evening in bed she spent a long time thanking the Lord for His care, protection and blessings He showered on her. She got out a pen and opened her prayer journal. *I am truly out of the crevice – out of that dark place where hope in things not seen is all I had. I didn't even feel I had a light to follow. I just kept putting my fears in the mud jar and leaving it all with Jesus. I asked for trust enough to carry me through and although each day was a renewed struggle to hold God's peace and resist my fears, in my weakness God's strength prevailed. I now see I can trust Him. Oh, I know my earthly mind will continue to press my spirit with doubts and fears, but I have my first success in a storm to look back on and say,* "God is with me. No one can defeat me." *Thank you for shelter and protection. Thank you for your guidance in controlling my behaviour. All crowns of praise given to me this day I lay at your feet.*

14 | Found Girl

The team flourished in Maya's absence. They worked efficiently in moving along the research. Sam and Kai found a slight temperature increase prior to the fertilization phase brought about a prolific and intense release of sperm and eggs within a span of a couple of days. Once the baby oysters reached the swimming phase, the introduction of a very small magnetic field along with a reduction in water turbulence, but steady water flow directing it to the intended anchor, effectively increased the success rate of fertilized eggs reaching adulthood from a few dozen of the 200 million eggs produced by one female in a season to several hundred.

Chris and Zach worked on developing cost-effective means to briefly and slightly warm the water near the adult oysters and introduce a slight magnetic field at the right time. They also worked on temporary environmental structures that would reduce the turbulence of waves, yet maintain a steady flow of water that would direct the swimming oysters to the intended anchors along the shoreline.

Once a week when Kai and Zach had kitchen duty, Chris and Sam had time alone and would meet on the upper deck to watch the sunset and talk of nonproject things. One warm evening they were reminiscing about the fun times in their college days. They reminded each other of several stories and laughed. They wondered what happened to some of their buddies. Sam reminded Chris of a beautiful blonde-haired beauty that turned his head toward the end of their final school year.

"What was her name? I don't remember her at all."

"I think her name was Cheryl or Sherry. You remember. She was the younger cousin of your roommate. She started hanging around during spring break. After a few weeks you two were inseparable."

"What? No, I don't remember anyone like that."

"Sure you do. She always referred to you as 'My Chris.' And was full of boundless energy."

"Oh yeah. I kind of remember her now. She always wore pink – pink lipstick, pink shirts, even pink pants. Yeah, yeah, I remember her. Man, it's been a long time since I thought about her."

"I kind of thought you two were destined for marriage."

"What? Pink-a-boo? Never!"

"Pink-a-boo?"

"Yeah, that's what we called her. No way. I was definitely not interested in her at all."

"Really? Why did you let her hang around so much if you didn't really like her?"

"I don't know. I guess I felt a bit sorry for her. She seemed kind of alone. I don't think other girls really liked her."

"Well, there was good reason for that. When you weren't around, she talked endlessly about herself, about how much you were interested in her, about your future together. She only thought about herself. She pushed the rest of us away."

"No, no, no. I had zero interest in her. My interest was definitely focused elsewhere. Say, I remember our friendship ended rather abruptly at the end of that school year. Whatever happened back then? You left so suddenly."

"I guess I thought it was time to move on and get a job."

"But you left without ever saying a word to me. You never said good-bye."

She looked down for a moment. "I landed a job in Ireland that start-ed almost immediately. I just had time to pack and go. I didn't think you would notice. I rather thought you were absorbed with Pink-a-boo."

"You broke my heart when you left, you know."

She shifted to look at him square on. "What do you mean, I broke your heart?"

He looked out to sea. "Yeah, I was bowled over by you. I thought about you all the time, even after you left."

"Well, how come you never let me in on the big secret?"

"I was shy. I guess I thought someone as great as you wouldn't want anything to do with me."

"What are you talking about? I was crazy about you and waited for you to ask me out. But when Pink-a-boo came along and talked endlessly about you and her, I thought you weren't interested in me and I moved on."

"So I was interested in you. You were interested in me. And we never realized it."

"And we both ended up with broken hearts."

Chris reached for her hand and held it on his lap. They were quiet for a long time.

"Sam, forgive me for letting you slip away. I see now with both Pink-a-boo and Maya that I let things happen around me – I should have been a man and dealt with them. I let my sympathies for these poor women who are anything but poor women lead me down paths I didn't wish to be on. Because of my inaction with you and with Pink-a-boo, you got away without ever knowing how I felt about you. It almost happened again with Maya."

He stood and pulled her up into his arms. "I make you this promise today. I will not let anyone come between us again. I've never let go of you in my heart. I was a fool for not chasing you down. That will not happen again. I'm overjoyed to have you back in my life. I can't tell you how much I thanked God for bringing you back to me. When I saw you again that first day in the hallway at the university, I didn't know if I was pushing my luck by pressing you into having dinner with me. But I didn't want to miss another chance with you. I was ecstatic when you came to the horse show and stayed for the evening. I've loved our times riding the trails. Then when you agreed to date, I guess I got careless. I let Maya's pathetic story cloud my thinking about what's right in how I handle my relationships. I know now I wasn't fair to you in my handling of Pink-a-boo and in my handling of Maya. I thought I was going to lose you again when NOAA forbid any correspondence with you all because I allowed Maya to think she had a hold on me. I promise you, I will allow nothing or no one to come between us again."

He held her face in his two hands. "Sam, I love you, my found girl. I never want to lose you again." He bent to kiss her. As she lingered in the kiss, he pulled her in close, holding her tight to him.

She held him tight. "I never want to lose you again either. And –" She leaned back to look at him. "I love you too. I've loved you for a very long time." She hugged him, resting her head on his shoulder.

15 | A Devastating Loss

Weeks and months passed. Soon phase 1 was complete. Kai and Zach returned to university. Chris and Sam presented their findings to NOAA, making recommendations of equipment and procedures that would quickly develop oyster reefs along the Louisiana coast. NOAA approved phase 2. Chris and Sam presented their recommendations to Louisiana's Department of Natural Resources. The state enthusiastically matched NOAA's funding and they were soon busy with the yearlong phase 2.

For that year Sam and Chris were inseparable. When the project completed, they celebrated their success with a big bash at Des Champs de la Baie. Kai and Zach came, along with all the folks they'd worked with at the Department of Natural Resources, the businesses that helped with the construction and all the volunteers.

The next evening Chris took Sam back to the restaurant where they had their first official date. They sat at the same table under the oak tree. Before dessert arrived Chris came to her side of the table and bent down on one knee. He took her hand in his. "Sam, my found girl. I have loved you for many years. I nearly lost you, letting you disappear. But God has put us back together. I've given you over a year now to get comfortable with me hanging around all the time. We spoke about you spending your life with me just so you can show me a picture of the old blacksmith shop when I'm old, to remind me of my nobility even in old age. Well, I don't want you to ever leave my side. I love you, Sam Morgan. And I promise to always love you, cherish you and value you above all others." He pulled out a jewellery box. "Sam Morgan, my found girl. Will you marry me? Will you be my wife into our noble old age?"

She held her hands to her mouth, eyes brimming with tears. She nodded and squeaked out a yes. He took the ring from the box and placed it on her finger. "It's called a fancy vivid blue diamond. That's its natural colour. I wanted a stone that would remind us of the ocean and the project that brought us back together. I liked this stone because it matches the colour of your eyes."

"It's beautiful. I love it." She held out her hand, looked at the ring on her finger, then pressed her left hand to her heart. "I love you so much." As she started to cry, she slipped off her chair and into his arms. He held her for a moment, then stood up with her still in his arms. He glanced back behind him and nodded. Music started.

She listened to the first few notes. "It's Love Is Blue – my mom's favourite." Her brows pressed together in concern. "This is a really sad song of love lost."

He smiled and began a slow dance. He whispered in her ear. "I rewrote the words." Quietly he sang.

"Blue, blue, the ocean blue,

Vast is my love, forever with you.

One, one, we'll be as one,

Dancing in joy for the life we've begun.

Sweet, sweet, my love is sweet,
Warm in my arms the morn we will greet.
Found, found, my lost girl found,
Until our death our souls will be bound .
Hold me now, how my bless'd heart sings,
Always love, through all that life brings."

When the music faded, she rested her head on his shoulder. "That was beautiful. I love those words. You've taken something so sad, so alone, and turned it into a lovely romantic song – our song. It's much like what you've done for the lost and alone me." They stood in each other's arms for a long moment. The waiter brought a bottle of dessert wine along with a heart-shaped strawberry dessert decorated with chocolate piping and the word love in caramelized sugar.

When they finished dinner, a limousine met them at the door and took them to the airport. They boarded a helicopter and flew out over the Gulf into the sunset. It dropped them off on a cruise ship with all their friends and family waiting to celebrate with them. The party went on into the wee hours of the morning. Then everyone went to their staterooms and slept as the ship made its way back to port.

It was a beautiful proposal, one she would never forget.

The following week while Sam and her mom were looking through wedding magazines, her mom excused herself. "I don't feel very good." Sam helped her to her bedroom. Jessie suddenly felt severe pain and had gone quite pale.

"I think you need to get to the hospital, Mom. I'm going to call the ambulance, okay?"

Her mom nodded.

After calling the ambulance she called her dad who was restocking the boat for the next charter. He told her to go in the ambulance and he'd meet them at the hospital. Sam felt sick to her stomach. The familiar worry of cancer hit her hard. While the ambulance attendants took her mom out to the vehicle, she called Chris. "It's Mom, Chris. We're just getting in the ambulance now. I'm really scared."

He promised to meet her at the hospital.

On the way the attendants gave Jessie a dose of morphine to help with the pain. It seemed to help a little bit, but she remained in significant pain. Sam held her cool hand. She could feel a sob coming and bit her lip and looked away until she could get her emotions under control. Jessie opened her eyes. "My dear, it's all in the hands of our God."

She wiped the brimming tears. "I know, but I don't want to lose you. You said you had a reassurance this was not your time."

"That was last time – over a year ago now. I'll tell you now what the Lord told me then. He said I would live to know the man you would marry. He promised to preserve me until you were settled with someone."

"But I'm not ready for this."

Her mom held her hand tightly. "Dear heavenly father, I thank you for a good life and that you've kept your promise to me. Thank you for giving my girl a wonderful man to be her husband. I would like to ask one more thing. Please come now and comfort Sam. She is one of your precious children and needs your loving presence to bind up her heart. Be with her and strengthen her. In your sweet name I pray, amen.

Jessie rested for a moment. Her breathing was shallow and fast. "Sam, listen to me. I've had a good life. God has been very good to me. If this is His time to take me, I'm ready to go. Don't mourn for me, as I know I'm going to a wonderful place. I will no longer suffer or be in pain. Honey, don't cry for me."

No longer trying to hold back her emotions, Sam sobbed openly. "I'm crying because I'm afraid to lose you. I love you, Mom. I don't want to let you go."

Her mom took several breaths before speaking. "You and I have all of eternity together. You will see me again."

I know, but that seems so long from now. I love you, Mom. You've been the best mom ever. And no matter what you say, I'm going to miss you so much. I don't know life without you. I'm not ready to let you go. But seeing her mom's exertion just to breathe Sam said, "Rest now, Mom. We're almost at the hospital." She stared out the windows at the passing buildings, trying to wrap her mind around what was happening.

When they entered the emergency department, Chris was waiting for her. The attendants moved Jessie to an examination room and onto the bed, leaving her in the care of the nurses. The same doctor from last time came within minutes. He ordered bloodwork and tests to confirm his suspicion of another ruptured blood vessel.

Brent arrived a few minutes later. After updating him she and Chris left her parents alone for a few minutes. They found a quiet hallway and she fell into his arms, sobbing deeply. "I'm not ready for her to die. I don't think I can do this. It's too hard. I love her too much to say goodbye."

He held her tightly and rubbed her back. He found them a couple of chairs to sit down. He held her hand. "I know you're in pain and I know I can't do anything to take it away, but I know God can help.

"Dear God, you can see the pain and grief in Sam. You know it comes from a love so deep. You are the only one who can reach into Sam's heart and hold it together. Only you can enter those deep places and pour your sweet healing into her. Lord, give us strength now to do what needs to be done and say what needs to be said. We turn Jessie over to your care. If this is her time to go home with you, we release her to you knowing she goes to a far better place and will wait for us there. In your abundance give us your peace, your courage and your strength. Help Sam let her mom go into your hands. In your name we pray, amen.

"Okay?"

She nodded.

"You need to be strong for her, Sam. If this is her time to go, you need to let her go in peace. You know Jesus will come and the second she draws her last breath, He will immediately take her spirit by the hand and together they will go to heaven. He will not allow her spirit to taste the evil of death. And she will finally be free of pain. That's a good thing, right?"

"I know. I'll be happy that she will finally be without pain. And I know we will be together again. It's awesome we have that hope, but that doesn't take away the pain of losing her now. My world has never been without her. I know I need to be strong for her now, and I will be. I just need to pull myself together."

Her dad came out. "They are going to take her to surgery. The cancer has aggressively returned and her liver has ruptured a large blood vessel. She has a severe internal bleed. You have a few minutes if you want to see her before they take her."

The three returned to the examination room. Her mom was visibly relieved to see her. She reached out her hand and Sam held it tightly. "They are going to try removing a section of my liver." She gasped for another breath. "I don't know if the Lord plans for me to come through this. Chris, promise you'll take care of my little girl."

He nodded. "I will."

"Sam, I've told the surgeon to not take any resuscitation measures." Sam was stunned.

Her mom took several short breaths. "The Lord has given me more days than was allotted to me. He preserved me until you met the love of your life who would fill the hole in your heart when I'm gone. He's fulfilled His promise, so I expect I will draw my last breath today."

"Mom, know I love you. I will always love you and there will always be a place in my heart reserved for you – always. No one will ever fill that spot. I understand what you're saying and I understand this is probably your time to go be with Jesus. I'll grieve for you, but I'll be okay. You're right. Chris will look after me. If this is your time to go, Mom, I release you to the care of Jesus. Chris and I prayed that He will be standing right here by your side, and when you draw your last breath, He will be right here to take you into His arms. I love you, Mom, so much." She held her mom's hand to her heart.

Jessie finally relaxed. She'd said all that was on her heart.

After a moment Sam said, "Mom, when you get to heaven and after you've greeted everyone you know, and you've had a big party, scout out some mansions close beside each other for all of us – something along the water. And tell God they are reserved for us. We'll be along soon enough. I know you're going to a better place and I know I'll be okay. And remember, I love you so much."

Jessie whispered through her tears, "I love you too." Her blood pressure suddenly plummeted. Alarms went off. Nurses hustled in. Jessie suddenly drew in a deep breath. Her eyes opened wide. She looked up. "Oh!" Her final breath escaped her lungs.

And then all was quiet, except for the steady monotone of the heartbeat monitor.

Sam sobbed. "Bye Mom. I love you."

Chris wrapped his arms around her. Brent's face was white. A single tear glided slowly down his cheek as he bowed his head.

The doctor rushed in and listened to her heart. He shook his head. "I'm sorry, but she's gone." He called her death. "Take as much time as you need."

The medical staff turned off the equipment, quietly withdrew and pulled the curtains closed behind them.

Brent leaned over and kissed his wife. "I love you, Jessie. You were the best wife a man could ask for. You can now rest in the peace of our Saviour. One of these days I'm coming and we will have eternity together. Love you, my sweet girl."

They were quiet for a long time as each one processed their thoughts. Sam felt like a part of her life had just been ripped from her. She knew and understood the great hope of all Christians, but that didn't make saying goodbye any easier.

Her heart ached with the loss. The grief came in waves, washing her under its consuming anguish. A blanket of sadness filled her mind. She couldn't see anything beyond her mother's death. She rested her head on the bed rail and wept. It was a sorrow deeper than losing Andrew. Tears streamed down her nose, steadily dropping to the floor. Grief crushed her heart with the weight of sorrow.

Chris gave her several tissues. She croaked out her thanks. Slowly the flood subsided. She lowered the rail and hugged her mom. She held on for a long time, then kissed her cool cheek. Grief washed over her anew. She sat back down sobbing. Eventually the tide of mourning eased again.

They lingered for several minutes, looking, touching and saying goodbye.

Finally Sam drew in a deep breath and held it for a moment. She let it go, stood up and said, "The valley of the shadow of death – we walked in as four people and leave with only three people." She bowed her head. "Jesus, look after her until we can all be together again." She looked at Chris. "It was just as you prayed. When she took her last breath, she saw Jesus."

16 | Standing on Leaving Lost

Chris drove Sam and Brent home. Brent took his Bible and went outside to be alone. Chris stayed through the evening. After hours of crying, Sam fell asleep on the couch in Chris' arms. He stayed until morning, not wanting to disturb her.

The following day was difficult for Sam. Everywhere she looked she saw reminders of her mother – the kitchen where she spent so much time, her shoes and coat in the closet, her chair at the table, her favourite teacup, her sweater draped over the sofa, her toothbrush in the bathroom, her purse at the door.

She expected the visitation and funeral to be equally difficult. Over her life she'd been to several, and had seen the broadcast of the funerals of famous people. She always marvelled at how the family held it together. She knew for her, all things related to her mom's funeral would be tough and that she didn't have the stoic emotional strength of most. She wasn't sleeping much and was increasingly exhausted. No amount of makeup would hide her pale, blotchy face and her swollen, bloodshot eyes. She didn't even bother trying.

She and Chris prayed for God's peace and strength to fill her heart and mind. And He was faithful in giving her a dose of fortitude. She gratefully managed all her conversations with a grace and composure she knew was not her own.

Chris' family attended both the evening visitation and the funeral. At a quiet moment Jenny and Alley spent a few minutes alone with Sam. Jenny gave her a warm hug. "If I can do anything, you let me know." She held her for a moment, looking into her eyes. Sam felt the world stand still. "You're part of our family now. I know I can't begin to fill your mother's shoes, but I think of you as my daughter. I love you, my dear. And I'm here for you, if you need." She hugged Sam again, holding her close.

Sam nodded with tears brimming. "Thank you."

Many people had made similar offers of "Anything I can do —" When Sam thought back over the day and the conversations, she kept going back to Jenny and when she looked into her eyes. She sensed she left something unsaid. Nonetheless, at that moment she felt the woman's deep compassion. At that moment she knew this woman loved her deeply.

The days passed slowly and with each one Sam struggled with grief that would suddenly roll in leaving her in a puddle of tears. But with each day it hit her less often and less intensely.

The day after the funeral, she asked Brent if she could have her mom's prayer journal. He smiled gently. "She told me you would want them."

"Them?"

He pulled a box out of the closet. She opened it to find a journal for every year. She looked at the journals for a moment, then looked at her father. He smiled. "She started these the first year we were married." He added her current one to the top of the stack. "She made sure I knew she wanted you to have these."

Unable to say much Sam nodded and squeaked out a thanks. She wasn't ready to read through them, but found it a great comfort to have them in her possession. She would put her hand on the stack and feel as though she was touching her mom's heart, the core of who she was. She could think of nothing more precious to receive from her.

A few weeks after the funeral, Sam called Jenny and asked if she could come see both her and Alley. They made arrangements for lunch the next day.

The next morning Sam gathered the collection of bridal magazines, brochures, and her file of notes she was making to organize her wedding, and put them all in a tote bag. When she arrived at Des Champs de La Baie she sat in the car for a moment. She took a deep breath. "I hope this goes well. I hope I'm right. I hope Jenny doesn't just do me this favour, but really jumps in." She grabbed her purse and the tote bag, and walked to the front door. "Lord, be with us today. Help this go okay." She rang the doorbell and Jenny answered.

She warmly hugged Sam and invited her in. Alley was already in the kitchen where a beautiful table was set. "Oh Jenny, you needn't have gone to such bother. This is beautiful. I can see where Chris gets his appreciation for fine dining."

"I wanted to make this special for you. Come. Sit down. Lunch will be ready in a moment."

Sam was grateful for light and easy conversation. Both Jenny and Alley let her choose the topic of conversation and they mostly chatted about things they were doing.

When they finished their lunch, Sam said, "I have a favour to ask of you two – well, mostly of you, Jenny. Mom and I had just started planning the wedding." She paused, gathering her courage. With the threat of tears, she said, "I find I'm in need of a mom to help me with all that goes into planning and organizing. If you are too busy or this is not your cup of tea, then please say so. I know this is a big favour to ask."

Jenny got up and pulled Sam into a long hug. "You are so special, so like your mom and so sweet. I would be honoured to help you. I can't begin to be your mom, but I will do my best. Oh Sam, thank you for asking." As they broke up the hug, they both sniffed back their tears.

"Okay, so here's as far as Mom and I got." She opened the magazines to the dresses she and Jessie liked. They talked over what the ceremony would be like, colours, bridesmaid dresses, flowers – and all things wedding. The three laughed and chatted excitedly for several hours.

When Sam headed home, she realized this was the first time since her mom's passing that she wasn't weighed down by her grief. The afternoon had gone so well. She'd been concerned that what she wanted and liked would be at odds with what they liked, but was quickly relieved of that worry when she discovered their tastes were very similar.

She and Jenny met every week. At first they focused on wedding plans, but as they became friends Sam found their friendship changed to one much like she had with her mom. One day she gave Jenny a pendant of silver with a pearl inside. "Mom and I found this when I was just a kid. She loved oysters and we'd gone out for lunch one day. She splurged and we both had oysters for lunch. In mine I found this pearl."

Jenny hesitated. "No, Sam. This is something you should keep to remember your mom."

"I really want you to have it. I always planned on having it made into a pendant and to give it to Mom before I married. I want you to have it because you've meant so much to me over the past weeks. This is but a small token of my feelings for you."

"Oh Sam." She wiped her eyes. "You have no idea what our friendship means to me. I wanted to let our relationship grow in its natural direction, but there's been something I've wanted to share with you for some time. I even thought about telling you at the funeral." She looked at the pendant in her hand, then closed her hand around it. "This seems like the right time.

"Back when Alley had her accident, I really struggled with understanding why God would do such a thing to my beautiful young girl. I was angry and confused. Then one day I asked Jessie out for lunch, and after a bit of chitchat I asked her how she could seemingly glide through life's trials with such unfailing faith in God. I knew I either had to find a way to peace and trust or it would be the end of me. She shared with me her secret. She told me of her journal in which she recorded her struggles and how God worked through them to bring good out of life's challenges. She called them her stones of faith.

"Since then, I too have recorded the difficult times, the things the Lord has said to me and all the evidence of His promises He's kept with me. She was right. I often go back and read all that the Lord has brought me through and I know my faith grows each and every time.

"I feel so privileged to fill in for her now until we all meet up again in heaven." She opened her hand and looked again. "I will treasure this. Thank you for letting me give back to you for all that your mom gave me."

That evening after Chris dropped her off, she thought about what Jenny said. *I wonder how many women Mom touched with her simple way to grow in their trust in God? How many women are living in God's abundant peace because she told about standing on her stones of faith?*

The evening before their wedding, she and Chris walked along Holly Beach to watch the sunset. They strolled hand in hand silently for several minutes. Finally he said, "Penny for your thoughts?"

"Sorry, I was thinking about something Mom left me. Since they were married she kept these journals of stones."

"What are journals of stones?"

"Stones are all life's challenges that confront us. Mom wrote about her difficult times and learned to watch for God's hand in bringing her through them. She noted how He turned all the bad stuff to something good. Then when another storm hit, she would read through all the previous times – all the documented demonstrations of God's faithfulness – and she then had trust enough for the day. She called them stones on her path, and when she'd lived through the crisis she said they became the rock foundation of her faith in God."

"That's what my mom does as well, although she doesn't call them stones of faith. I like that bit."

She laughed slightly. "Your mom told me she got the idea from my mom a few years ago. Anyway Mom told Dad to give me all her journals. He pulled out a boxful from the closet."

"Have you read them?"

"Not yet. I thought since she wrote them starting when they were first married, I would start reading them after we are married – ouch!" She hopped on one foot and looked back in the sand to see what she'd stepped on.

Chris picked up a most unusual blue and purple iridescent chunk of metal. He dusted it off and turned it over. "It's crystallized bismuth. If cooled in a particular way, it crystallizes into these stacks of rectangles. Someone must have lost it. Funny it ended up here." He handed it to her.

She looked at it for a long time. "It reminds me of my journey to overcome the stone – or rather boulder – on my path. For the last two years in Scotland, I mourned Andrew's passing. I let my grip on this world loosen. At first I grieved over the loss of him, but then in time that shifted to mourning the loss of all the things I imagined could have been had he lived. I became lost in that illusion. Mom soon straightened me out and I recommitted my life to living God's way. I called my first stone Leaving Lost. It had a few dark crevices and some pointy bits, but just as Mom said, God brought me through and now I have you. This chunk of metal is like Leaving Lost – big and unyielding with deep valleys."

"Then I think it was here for you to find and keep."

Distractedly she said, "Yes." She rinsed it in the water then rested it on her flat hand. "Yes, this is Leaving Lost." Pointing to the highest rectangle, she said, "And here I am standing on top. I can see the beauty of the stone now. Oh, it had hard parts. And dark parts. And parts where I couldn't see any light. But now I'm on top and in the sunlight. And I can see the wonderful, even exquisite appearance of Leaving Lost now that I've reached the top. You're right. I'll keep this as a memento of my first boulder of faith."

Before going to bed she set her memento on top of the plastic container of mud.

She remembered her mother talking about being in the Land of Lost and the misery of having no hope. *What were Mom's exact words? "When you're pining for lost things, you will find yourself a castaway in a sea of hopelessness."*

Lost. Yes, it is a dark place to live when there is no hope. I can now look back and see the beautiful evidence of your faithfulness, God. Thank you for carrying me through the hard times. I now see your hand of provision, your strength and your peace. I would have stumbled on my own. I wouldn't have found my way through to the top. Thank you, Lord, for giving me a beautiful and real life to look forward to. Help me let go of all the future lost days with Mom, and remember her without the heavy mantle of grief. Help make my wedding a celebration.

She looked at the stone sitting on top of the mud container. *It isn't right to keep looking at all my fears. I think it's time to get rid of the mud. All the fears have been removed and the mud is now an ugly distraction from God's beautiful provision. I'll take it out to the Big Lake tomorrow and wash it clean.*

She moved the metal chunk to her night table and sat on her bed looking at it. *Today, I stand in the bright sunshine. I'm filled with hope and bathed in your glorious iridescent light. Thank you for helping me on my journey of faith. I can say with James I count it all joy when the troubles came my way. Because of you I stand this day an overcomer.* She lightly touched the metal.

"Thank you, God, for giving me courage. Thank you for building my faith. I did ask that you would make Leaving Lost a stone of faith. And Mom said that any stone that builds faith would not be easy. I see now you used a trial of metal, not stone, to build precious metal in me – metal of gold and silver that won't burn away in your refining fire.

"Thank you for bringing me out of Lost. Thank you for an amazing man that I'll marry tomorrow. I invite your presence tomorrow, and in our marriage for the rest of our lives. Thank you for a wonderful woman who can fill in for Mom tomorrow and for the remainder of her days. Thank you for showing me the hidden beauty of trials – to come to the place where I can count it joy. Thank you for building my faith.

"Thank you for the experience of Leaving Lost."

Epilogue

Sam awoke to bright sunshine. *My wedding day.*

Stephanie, her best friend and maid of honour had arrived from Scotland a couple of days before for the rehearsal and dinner. She had secretly organized for Sam to have something old, something new, something borrowed and something blue.

When Sam and Jessie started planning her wedding, she thought she would like to get married in her mom's dress, but she was much taller than her mom and there was not enough material to lengthen it. After her mom passed, she decided to incorporate the lace into a modern-styled dress for herself – something old and something new.

On the morning of her wedding, she and Stephanie met Jenny and Alley at the hairdresser. Sam arranged an appointment with Guy, the town's wedding hairdresser. She wanted a professional to do something with her long and unmanageably curly hair. He pulled it back loosely into a carefree combination of curls and braids at the back topped with a back headband of lace and pearls.

When ready to leave Jenny tried to give Sam the pearl pendant she had given her.

Sam initially refused it. "Oh no, I wanted you to keep this. I always intended it for my mom for this day. And now that's you."

Jenny smiled. "My dear, this is something borrowed for you to have for today. When Stephanie called to ask me for something you could borrow, I knew the pearl you intended for your mom would be particularly meaningful for you – a little memory to carry with you today."

She accepted it with tears brimming in her eyes. "Thank you. This is so special."

"You can attach it to your bouquet as I understand from Stephanie you already have a necklace to wear."

"So Steph says. I haven't seen it yet."

"Well then best you two get on your way. You don't want to be late for your wedding."

She bent and kissed Jenny on the cheek. "Thank you for everything."

Stephanie and Sam hurried home to get ready. Stephanie helped her with her dress, then gave her a gift from Chris. "He wanted to give you something blue."

"Have you seen what it is?"

"I've seen photos, but not the real thing."

Sam opened the wrapping paper and the jewellery box. Chris had bought a beautiful white and blue diamond necklace and blue diamond drop earrings. "These are stunning. They go perfectly with my ring." She put them on and looked at herself in the mirror.

Stephanie sighed, "You are the most beautiful bride ever. Chris is going to be wowed by you today."

Sam hugged her friend. "You are too kind. Thank you so much for coming all this way for me. And thank you for arranging all these things to make my day special."

"I have one more thing. This one is from me. The full saying is, 'Something old, something new, something borrowed something blue and a silver sixpence for your shoe.' Here's a silver sixpence."

"You are a gem." She hugged Stephanie. "I couldn't have anyone better standing with me today."

They arrived at the church a few minutes ahead of time. Steph helped with last-minute primping then stood at the back of the church to head down the aisle with the best man. The church had three sections of pews – one middle and two sides. Sam glanced at the front row of the middle section for Jenny. She was glad for the layout of the church. Jenny had filled in for her mom and appreciated that Jenny now sat in the middle of the pew – between the bride and groom's side of the church.

When Sam started down the aisle she looked at Chris. He smiled and winked at her. She greeted friends and family as she made her way to the front. Once at Chris' side he said, "You are so beautiful, my found girl. Your mom would be proud of you today."

"Thanks Chris. You're pretty spectacular yourself."

She looked down at her bouquet. She had carefully placed the pearl pendant and her Leaving Lost iridescent metal piece where she could see them among the flowers. *I'm here living out my most wonderful day because of Mom and God.* She squeezed Chris' hand and he squeezed back.

Thank you, God, for a mom that loved you and taught me to follow you in trust. Thank you for your courage and strength. I would have remained lost in my fairy tales. I would have been lost in finding a way out of the trouble stirred up by Maya. And I would have been lost when Mom left this world to be with you. But I've journeyed out of Lost. Standing on the pinnacle only happened because Mom showed me the way and you led me through the storms. In joy I thank you, God, for Leaving Lost.

The
END

Leaving Lost

Thank You

If you've enjoyed *Leaving Lost* please leave a review, tell a friend or send the author a note. Your review will help other readers decide on this book!

To be notified of upcoming releases new books sign up at SerenityMcLean.com/author-updates/ And anyone interested in reading an advance copy of a book before its release in exchange for an honest review can sign up at SerenityMcLean.com/author-updates/

You can also visit SerenityMcLean.com for her full list of great fiction.

Leaving Lost

What's Next

Book One of the Glass Darkly series, *Memory of Memories*

Astonishing. Exquisite. Sublime.

Lani spent her whole life wondering what life after death would be like when heaven deluged her senses with an experience far richer than she had ever imagined.

Upon her arrival in heaven she received her new name Aha'Lani, a weaver of stories of what was, is, and is yet to come. At first Lani puzzled over carrying a name of story teller. She sketched, painted and sculpted, but never considered herself a writer or storyteller. How can this be? Yet the seeds of desire planted inside her from youth, left unrealized in life, had an eternal purpose beyond her earthly imagination.

She soon sees her eternal journey will abundantly fulfill her heart's desires – desires of born in her youth. All came together in a powerful eternal mission. And all this in an unimaginable place.

Have you wondered what heaven will be like? Read this book if you are curious to peer into the potential of eternal life of complete fulfillment, satisfaction, and more real than anything this earth offers.

Buy *Memory of Memories* to peer into what your future will be like in heaven – imagine big!

What Readers Have Said

This story contains such rich descriptions of places, feelings, sights so that you really feel you are there. ~ Catherine Orfald

This novel is the book version of a warming cup of tea on a cold day; it is a comforting read that gives that warm feeling that continues to radiate long after you have finished. ~ Gemma

I found [this book] to be well written...and creative. The characters are believable, the writing descriptive...Good for a believer, or an open-minded questioner. ~ Lynne

I really enjoyed reading this unusual tale. It was written beautifully. You may think it is a crazy idea behind the story, but it is a lovely story, with depth and qualities that inspire. ~ Lilian Flesher

Totally impressed with this eloquently written novel. ~ Monica

It was a unique perspective and begs the reader to consider what will eternal life be like. It's an interesting take on the subject and well worth reading. ~ Nese Ellyson

Story Opening

I celebrate in the ocean,
I dance in joy.
I sing in delight.
I laugh in paradise.
Celebrate life.

Lani read the date and poem and smiled. In the long past she hadn't considered herself a writer or storyteller. In fact, she never kept a journal or diary, but in her first year here, she found…

Read about an extraordinary life in heaven! *Memory of Memories* is now available both as paperback and ebook on Amazon.

The Flawless Life

Prequel to the Glass Darkly series

Desperate. Grappling with her faith. And hope in things unseen.

Grace's world was shaken when she lost her job. There was a first rush of concerns: How can she survive? She had her mother to look after. What will she tell her? Does God even know her circumstances? What started as an initial voice of anxiety and a sickening feeling had rapidly become a choir of condemnation and overwhelming fear and despair.

Now struggling in her Christian walk, Grace found herself tired to the core, and weary of running the good race. Life had been hard and now it felt even her heart had been stripped out of her, leaving a shell of the person she was in her youth. The blackness of despair closed in.

In a whispered breath, "You are flawless in my eyes" and a flood of understanding shook her very being. The truth – the core truth broke through her barriers and reached deep inside. It gripped her heart, confronted her mind. The brilliant light of truth shattered the chains of condemnation and guilt. How could she not have understood the obvious truth? The simple truth demolished her defences, blew her mind, smashed her bonds, and transformed her life.

If you are interested in a story of flourishing in a life crisis then this book is for you.

Buy *The Flawless Life* now and walk the path of carefree and flawless!

Selected Excerpts

Now the landscape of her heart lay stripped bare, and the beach of her mind left barren except for the inevitable scraps of damage strewn everywhere. That wave emptied her soul of emotion. All washed out to sea. She felt like a hollow shell. Depleted. Desolate. Drained.

He says he has walked away from yesterday and tomorrow, and simply lives in this moment's grace. He's committed to a life where he dances in joy, loves, shares life, and leaves the burden of religion at the cross and the heavy lifting of worry and pain to God.

Just because I cannot see into tomorrow, I know the creator of all took care of it long ago. It is finished, already done. I didn't need to plead and beg Him to action. No, He already provided, it is finished. And He requires no circus of performance from me – just trust and faith. All the chaos and stress, all my failed effort – not required? What a relief!

Story Opening

Experienced, they operated quickly. They ripped the bandage off in a matter of seconds, leaving her reeling. They walked her back to her office to gather her purse. The rest would be boxed up and sent to her. They collected her security cards and escorted her out the door. Done. Within ten minutes they completed their deed.

At the elevators she stood. Alone. Jobless.

Read about how the sharks of life seeking to destroy us can become turtles! *The Flawless Life* is now available both as paperback and ebook on Amazon.

Weeping Dune

From the Heartwarming and Inspiring Series

Escape. Alone. Rising courage. And a life transformed.

In a crisis Jules was faced with a decision – stay and accept Anders' fist or run and face an uncertain future.

She ran. By coincidence or divine intervention she found herself back in the warm arms of South Carolina.

She faces her longstanding feelings of worthlessness. She discovers the people of this small town know a secret of her past kept quiet for a couple of generations – a secret that will rock her world and change the course of her future forever. And she stumbles upon a hidden tribute that seems to be written as an expression of her thoughts and feelings as she has them.

Jules soon discovers life in a beach town looks deceptively sleepy, but for her it is filled with excitement. Every day she moves further and further from her old life. In the end she wears the beach captured in a stone around her neck and the heart of the sea on her hand.

Walk with Jules as she finds the happiness and courage of her youth, and discovers so much more! Buy *Weeping Dune* now and learn its secrets!

Selected Excerpts

I've cried for love in the vast emptiness and it just absorbed my pleas. The silence there was deafening. It offered no relief.

Aloneness isn't just the physical absence of others. It has a voice that speaks directly to the heart. My eyes see people everywhere, yet I only see blackness inside. Ears hear laughter and love all around, but my internal being only hears the resounding echo of loneliness. Today I saw the sun, felt its warmth on my skin. I saw the unceasing waves bubbling and heard their gurgling laughter. Yet my soul doesn't match the life around me. I fear walking through life alone. I fear the emptiness, the blackness. The overwhelming silence of alone.

What awaits me here – this place of sky, sea and sand? I'd forgotten how much I loved warm summer nights and the smell of saltwater. I feel like I've finally come home. A home I haven't known for over half my life.

He holds you in His hand where life and love flourish. Are you going to let your past without God stop you from enjoying all He wants to give you?

"I am not even a whisper away. Always."

Story Opening

She hid in the dark bathroom, sobbing. Waiting. Listening. Quiet finally ruled the hotel room for at least an hour. She came to a decision. Cowering in the darkness gave her plenty of time to think. She finally had enough. The rocky relationship had crossed her line. Anders scared her. Now she needed to wait until he fell into a drunken sleep to quietly slip away.

Read about how God can restore what life's locusts have eaten! *Weeping Dune* is now available both as paperback and ebook on Amazon.

Rainswept

From the Intriguing Expedition Series

Mystery. Epidemic disaster. And romantic intrigue.

A trail of unexplained deaths and impending environmental collapse lead a beautiful scientist to the shores of the Baja, a suspicious surfer, and a long overdue confrontation with her sister.

Coming in 2016!

Leaving Lost

Never Midnight

From the Heartwarming and Inspiring Series

Betrayed. Deserted. Determined to keep life at a distance.

Leigha grew up in a happy home with a loving mom who had become her best friend. During her first year in college her mom was diagnosed with terminal cancer and decided not to tell Leigha. When her mom passed away Leigha felt angry, betrayed and deserted, and refused to deal with her grief. Over the years she knew the darkness of grief's valley of the shadow of death waited for her to enter and pass through as many have before her. Yet she still harboured her feelings of betrayal and worthlessness.

Running from her grief and her memories Leigha hid herself for years in the faceless crowd of a large metropolis. Slamming the door on her past she settled on two life rules – don't go home and don't get emotionally involved.

With one urgent phone call she decided to break one rule. For five years the black chasm called grief waited patiently for her and now the time had come to face her anger and loss. She soon discovered a treasure left behind by her mom. She learned the truth of her mother's final days on this earth and the love that left behind a treasure. It changed her perspective and brought forgiveness.

And before she realized, she was well on the way to breaking her second rule.

If you enjoy a story of reconciliation, and love then pick it up for free now!

Story Opening

She recalled the day she left for college. She was so excited. Her life had been a fairy tale – a happy childhood filled with love, learning and life. She grew up in a loving home, in a safe community, and on an exceptionally beautiful island that invited her daily to explore every part of the island. When young, she and her mother were inseparable adventurers. As she grew up, her mother had become a trusted friend. Her mother taught her to love the land, love the water and love the potential of each day. She'd dearly loved her mom. She was an exceptional woman who opened her eyes to a world full of things to learn, people to engage, and opportunities to investigate. Leaving for college seemed a big exciting step into a world of exciting options. That day she'd hugged her mom goodbye silently thanking her for showing her a world of possibilities.

Like people remembering where they were and what they were doing when Kennedy was assassinated or when the World Trade Towers collapsed, she remembered the day, the hour, the very moment when she heard her mother had passed away. It was the ground zero juncture when her world exploded apart. The clarity of the memory brought with it a biting sting.

Read about coming through life's tough circumstances on top!

Never Midnight is now available for free at serenitymclean.com/never_midnight_promo/

Message From Serenity

These times of economic and political world unrest can be unsettling. But God doesn't want our lives to be filled with fear. Thankfully He made provision for us to not be fearful despite the frightful events around us. The Bible tells us to think on things of goodness.

> *And now, dear brothers and sisters, one final thing. Fix your thoughts on what is true, and honorable, and right, and pure, and lovely, and admirable. Think about things that are excellent and worthy of praise (Philippians 4:8).*

I hope you found yourself thinking about God, your relationship to Him and your walk with Him while reading this book. What we do in this life sets us up for our eternal life. Invest your spare time thinking on the things of heaven. Keep your eyes fixed on that eternal light at the end of the valley of darkness.

Look up. I can't help but be excited by the thoughts of our inheritance and eternal life with our Maker. I love that we are told to think about heaven. Just know it is bigger and better than anything you can imagine.

In the meantime, imagine big and keep reading!

Leaving Lost

About the Author

Serenity, born in Ontario, now lives in Western Canada. Like the main character Serenity spent many, many hours thinking about eternity and what it would be like. This inspired The Glass Darkly series.

While writing *Memory of Memories* and *The Flawless Life*, she looked forward to the next book in the series, but God had other plans and inspired several stand alone books while she continues her research for the third book in the series, *The Omega Ages*.

As a "pantser" author (writing by the seat of her pants), she doesn't start with an outline, but simply writes the story. When she set out to write this story, she knew the main character would finally confront her feelings about her mother's passing and come back into relationship with God. But as seems to be the way with her writing, she met the characters as they entered the story. And she discovered the role they'd play as the story unfolded.

"I don't know if there are many authors like me, but I close my eyes and the story plays out like a video in my head. Then I write the story of what I've seen."

You can read more about Serenity on her website at www.serenitymclean.com/info/.

On her website Serenity provides more detail on each of her books. (You can read a full chapter in the Books section.) There are several short stories you can read for free in the Short Stories and Bonus Content section. Readers of purchased books can gain access to bonus content – extra chapters extending the story. If you've really enjoyed Serenity's stories you can sign up to become a book reviewer and receive advanced copies of her new releases.

Visit her blog to read posts on topics including current events and future musings. Follow Serenity on Twitter as she tweets and exchanges thoughts with her followers. Finally, connect with Serenity on her Facebook page.

Get in touch as she loves to talk about her books, current events and the prophetic timeline.

She looks forward to hearing from you.

Connect with Serenity:

Blog: www.serenitymclean.com/blog/

Twitter: twitter.com/SerenityMclean_ (note the underscore at the end)

Pinterest: www.pinterest.com/mclean3963/

Facebook: www.facebook.com/Serenityauthor

YouTube: www.youtube.com/channel/UCt82lzlc7NDixFAHfuFZXfg

Instagram: www.instagram.com/serenitymclean_/

JD Farag

JD is my online pastor living in Kaneohe, Hawaii. You can find him at www.youtube.com/user/alohabibleprophecy. He is a wonderfully honest and humble guy teaching on the entire Bible. He delivers an important message of hope in these days of global unrest and uncertainty. Each week he uploads videos from his Thursday Bible study, the Sunday service and the Prophesy Update to his YouTube channel. All are great and well worth watching.

If you are wondering *if* you are going to heaven, JD has a good news message for you.

The Good News of Salvation in Jesus Christ

The good news of salvation in Jesus Christ is also known as the Gospel, which means good news, your debt has been paid in full and you've been set free. However, in order for the good news to be good, there must also be bad news to make that good news good. Thus we need the bad news first. So what's the bad news? Thankfully, the Bible is not silent concerning both the bad news and the good news.

The Bad News

Romans 3:10. As it is written: "There is no one righteous, not even one...

Romans 3:23. ...for all have sinned and fall short of the glory of God...

Romans 5:12. Therefore, just as sin entered the world through one man, and death through sin, and in this way death came to all people, because all sinned...

Romans 6:23a. For the wages of sin is death...

John 3:3. Jesus replied, "Very truly I tell you, no one can see the kingdom of God unless they are born again."

The Good News

Romans 6:23b. ...but the gift of God is eternal life in Christ Jesus our Lord.

Romans 5:8. But God demonstrates his own love for us in this: While we were still sinners, Christ died for us.

Romans 10:9–10. If you confess with your mouth, "Jesus is Lord," and believe in your heart that God raised him from the dead, you will be saved. For it is with your heart that you believe and are justified, and it is with your mouth that you profess your faith and are saved.

Romans 10:13. "Everyone who calls on the name of the Lord will be saved."

When you fully understand the bad news, you'll want to hear the good news and call on the name of the Lord, confessing with your mouth that "Jesus is Lord," and believing in your heart that God raised Him from the dead. Then, if and when you do this, the Bible promises you will be saved and have everlasting life.

John 3:16. For God so loved the world that he gave his one and only Son, that whoever believes in him shall not perish, but have eternal life.

Here is an example of how you can call on the Lord and accept Jesus

Christ's payment for your sin, which He paid for in full with His death on the cross and His resurrection from the dead:

"Dear Lord Jesus, I know I am a sinner. I believe in my heart that You died for my sins, and I confess with my mouth that you rose again from death. I accept you as my Lord and Savior. Thank you for saving me. Amen."

Again, this is only an example of how you can call on the Lord and be saved. This is the most important decision you will ever make. When you make this decision, the Holy Spirit will indwell you and empower you to live a holy life. Then, when He does, you will find you no longer desire the things of your old life. Instead, you'll have a desire to read the Bible, which is the Word of God, and you'll also desire to go to church and fellowship with the people of God, this because you are now born again of the Spirit of God.

Thanks, JD!

If you have accepted Jesus Christ's payment for your sins and now live with Him as your Lord and saviour, both JD and I will see you in heaven! Remember no eye has seen, no ear has heard, nor has it entered into the imagination of any human the great things in store for those who belong to Him. Think big because it will be better than that!

Leaving Lost

Leaving Lost

www.ingramcontent.com/pod-product-compliance
Lightning Source LLC
Chambersburg PA
CBHW071252130626
46556CB00003B/1284